My Dearest Reagan

Cowboy Crossing
Book 7

Jessie Gussman

Contents

Acknowledgments

Cover art by Julia Gussman
Editing by Heather Hayden
Narration by Jay Dyess
Author Services by CE Author Assistant

———

Listen to the unabridged audio for FREE performed by Jay Dyess on the Say with Jay channel on YouTube. Get early access to all of Jay's recordings and listen to Jessie's books before they're available to the general public, plus get daily Bible readings by Jay and bonus scenes by becoming a Say with Jay channel member.

In Appreciation

I've been blessed with an amazing ARC team. So many talented people who help to keep me straight and make my books accurate and worth reading. I owe them more than I can ever repay.

For this book, I needed a little specialized help with Gladys's surgery, and I would like to thank Nati Hurtado for her willingness to spend some extra time on my manuscript and use her expertise from her day job as a veterinary surgeon to help me make sure my details were accurate. Nati has been an ARC reader for a long time, and I consider her a friend. Maybe we'll meet someday. ☺

As always, any mistakes or inaccuracies are mine alone.

Chapter One

Reagan Boyle looked up as the bell above the veterinary clinic door chimed, and a blast of cold air ripped through the waiting room, ruffling her papers.

She put a hand down to make sure her papers didn't blow away, but she did not, not for one second, wish she was back at her place of previous employment, which had been completely paperless.

Some things weren't worth it.

"It looks like Toto has a clean bill of health, Mrs. Hudson," Reagan said as she handed the receipt to Mrs. Hudson.

She smiled at Toto and patted the miniature poodle mix on the head around the tuft of fur tied up with a pink ribbon as she poked out of Mrs. Hudson's over-the-shoulder dog carrier/purse.

Mrs. Hudson set her checkbook down on the shelf and began writing. Many of their older clients still wrote checks, even though they encouraged electronic payments.

"He sure does. It's a nice report to get," she said as she scribbled on the paper. Her head turned to the left, and Reagan turned her head with her. Whoever was coming in hadn't made it past the doorway yet.

Often animals, especially dogs, didn't like to walk into the office without sniffing for a long time in the doorway.

Reagan didn't think too much of it.

"I have to admit, Mrs. Hudson, you don't seem like the kind of person who would have a designer dog in her purse to carry around. I could see you with a more practical dog. A good German Shepherd, maybe."

Maybe she couldn't have said that to another lady, but Mrs. Hudson seemed like the kind of woman a person could say anything to.

"I think my boys bought him for me as a kind of practical joke. Not that they think that animals are jokes, exactly, and they knew I would love him. But you're right, this is not the kind of dog that I would have chosen." Her work-roughened hand stroked over the dog's head while the pink tongue came out and licked her worn fingers. "But I can't say that Toto hasn't brought me a good bit of comfort, with Mr. Hudson being diagnosed with pancreatic cancer just a week ago."

"You're kidding?" Reagan said, truly horrified. Mr. Hudson was a pillar in the community of Cowboy Crossing, and everyone knew him. She had to add, "I just saw him last week at the grocery store, and he seemed fine."

"He's just been feeling a little under the weather and had some pain. It was a shock. But we're going to fight it. Of course." Mrs. Hudson wrote her check out, and her voice was matter-of-fact, not that Reagan would expect anything different from the sturdy stock of Cowboy Crossing. Missourians were descended from the tough folks who tamed the West. They were most definitely proud, independent, and very capable.

Mrs. Hudson epitomized the soul of that.

"Of course." Reagan put her hand on her stomach, pressing the material of her sweatshirt closer. The temperature in the room had dropped since the door was still half open. Thankfully the wind was no longer blowing her papers.

"My goodness, it's chilly outside for the middle of November," Mrs. Hudson said, tucking her checkbook back in the pocket of her purse and patting Toto's pink-ribboned head.

"I'm sorry to hear about Mr. Hudson. If there's anything I can do..." Reagan's voice trailed off. She could barely take care of herself and her little brother. In fact, she needed a place to rent. She was moving out of her apartment in Trumbull, since she quit her job at the vet clinic there.

Thankfully her lease was up, because the place she was renting was more than she could afford. Not to mention the commute was longer than she liked.

Ideally, she'd like to find a place closer to her new job so Dylan, her younger brother, was closer to her. She'd had custody of her brother since she turned eighteen, not long after their dad had been sent to prison for his third DUI.

Her older brothers had offered to take him, but they were working hard on getting the ranch that they owned jointly up and running, and Reagan had felt she would be a steadier influence.

That was laughable. After the massive mistake she'd made seven months ago, she wasn't any better influence than anybody else in Dylan's life. She should have let their older brothers take him.

Too late for that now.

"Thank you so much, sweetie, I'll definitely take you up on that if I need you." Mrs. Hudson adjusted the strap on her shoulder. Her tone was sweetly thankful, making Reagan feel like her offer—as little as it was—was deeply appreciated. "Actually, if you don't mind keeping an eye on Toto right now while I carry this dog food out to my car, that would be a help."

Mrs. Hudson's eyes sparkled, and she didn't look like a woman whose husband had just been diagnosed with a cancer that probably had one of the highest death rates of any he could have gotten. She looked just as happy and serene as she always had. And she knew how to make Reagan feel better. Because, yeah, there wasn't much she could do, but she could babysit a dog for five minutes and feel like a help.

"Hang on one second; let me come around."

There was a door at the side she had to go out, and while she was walking to it, she heard a deep voice say, "Mrs. Hudson, I'll get that dog food for you, if that girl will hold my dog. Her name's Gladys." The man added the last sentence almost sounding sheepish, like he was a little ashamed of the name.

Reagan had come around the corner, and at Mrs. Hudson's smile and nod, she continued on to take the leash the man held out.

She didn't recognize the guy. She wouldn't call him exactly handsome, but he was striking.

Not his looks maybe, but the way his eyes seemed to slam into her as he tilted his head and they became visible under his cowboy hat.

Intelligent eyes, with a confident bearing, and a body that looked like it was used to physical activity.

He didn't specifically look like a rancher to her, but she couldn't put her finger on why not.

She tore her eyes away, fastening them on the first thing she found, which happened to be his dog, even as she took the leash from him, and their fingers brushed.

She completely ignored any sensation that might be traveling up her arm.

She already made that mistake seven months ago when she'd been caught by magnetic eyes and mistaken lust for love.

Her bad.

But she did not need to make the same mistake twice.

Even if similar consequences were impossible in her current situation.

In her peripheral vision, the man jerked his head. "Thanks."

He walked to Mrs. Hudson and picked up the bag of dog food at her feet. "This is an awful lot of dog food for that little dog to be eating."

Mrs. Hudson's laugh rang out, the kind of laugh that sounded like she wasn't afraid to laugh and wasn't afraid for anyone to hear. The kind of laugh that made anyone listening want to smile along with her. It just sounded so happy.

"He's not the only dog out on the ranch. One of them has a delicate stomach and needs to have this special blend."

"I see." The man paused with the bag slung over his shoulder. "How'd you find out that your dog had a delicate stomach?"

Mrs. Hudson's face glowed with humor. "Every time after she ate, every time, she threw up. We couldn't get her to stop. So we brought her here. Dr. Violet suggested we put her on a more bland diet. That did the trick, and she's been fine ever since. We're kind of afraid to change her back, although Dr. Violet said it's probably okay. A lot of times, puppies' stomachs are just a little sensitive for a period."

"Yeah, sounds a little like what Gladys is going through. I'll make sure I say something to the doc during my visit." He eyed the dog connected to the leash Reagan was holding. It was a beautiful German Shepherd, golden with black highlights, but she huddled against Reagan's leg like she was scared to death. Not uncommon in the vet's office, and her eyes never left the man. She strained a little against the leash like she wanted to be with him, even as she cowered behind Reagan.

She did seem a little underweight too. Although her fur was thick and beautiful, and there were no ribs visible through it.

"You do that. I'm sure Dr. Violet will fix you right up," Mrs. Hudson said as the man adjusted the bag of dog food and turned toward the door.

Mrs. Hudson hurried around and opened it for him, holding it. But instead of walking out to her car, she came back to the doorway.

"Reagan?" she asked softly. "I believe Dr. Violet told me that you were looking for a place to stay. If you check on this board," she indicated the bulletin board that was right beside the door when a person walked in, "it looks like there's a couple of offers here." Her brows lifted, and her face kind of lowered as her voice came out in more of a warning tone. "Just be careful. If you want one of my boys to check it out for you before you go by yourself, you just let me know. Cowboy Crossing is a very safe place, but bad people are everywhere."

"I'll do that," Reagan said, fingering the leash, knowing she wouldn't want to put anyone out, but also knowing Mrs. Hudson was right.

"Mrs. Hudson!" a voice called as an exam room door opened and closed. "I heard you were in here. Just hold on a second. I want to talk to you... I heard about your husband."

Mrs. Hudson smiled and walked past Reagan to the lady who was calling her. They hugged each other, and Reagan looked away.

She hadn't been around Cowboy Crossing long enough to feel comfortable hugging anyone. That wasn't the fault of anyone in Cowboy Crossing; it was her own. She hadn't gotten out nearly as much as what she wanted to, or should have, since she started working here six months ago.

Gladys whined at her legs, and Reagan stroked between those tulip-shaped ears. Maybe if they got a stable home, if she found a great place to rent, they could afford to get a small dog. Dylan had been begging for one...

She probably shouldn't be thinking about getting a dog. She had other responsibilities to think about.

Shifting her bulky sweatshirt, glad that she worked for a vet who didn't require her to dress up, she shuffled toward the bulletin board, careful not to step on Gladys who huddled against her legs and shuffled along with her.

To read the board, she had to stand right in front of the door, but thankfully it opened in the opposite direction, so no one would smash into her when they walked in.

There were two cars for sale, a motorcycle, free kittens, and seven horses. No houses for rent.

Her heart dropped. She needed to find something.

But that's what she'd been running into everywhere she looked. There just weren't any places in Cowboy Crossing.

She had a little less than a week to move out of her current place.

If she absolutely had to, she could move in with her brothers. But they were almost just as far outside of Cowboy Crossing in the opposite direction as her current place in Trumbull. Dylan wouldn't be any closer, and her commute wouldn't be any shorter. Plus, she didn't want to be a burden to her older brothers. They were fighting hard to start something from scratch. She couldn't help them—not with taking care of Dylan and the new little one, but she could keep them from having to take responsibility that would draw them away from what they were working on.

Their family hadn't exactly been the kind of family where the parents had launched the children into the world well prepared, with plenty of financial and emotional resources behind them.

They'd been kind of dropped on their heads into their lives.

She wanted something different for Dylan. And for the baby that she would have soon.

She put another hand on her stomach.

She'd made a mistake, but her baby wasn't a mistake.

Unfortunately, it seemed she was destined to repeat the mistakes of her parents, because she wasn't exactly bringing this child into a stable home. She was no more ready to bring up a child and launch them into the world than her parents had been.

Except, her child would have love. All the love she could give it. She would make sure of that.

Whatever else happened, her baby would never wonder whether there was anyone in the world who loved her.

Her brother wouldn't either. Dylan was such a great kid. He didn't deserve to feel unloved, even for a second. No child did.

She wouldn't wish her childhood on anyone.

The door opened with a blast of cold air, and Reagan whirled, crossing her arms over her chest and hugging them to herself.

The striking man had walked back in. She wanted to back up, to get away from him, but Gladys cowered behind her legs, pushing and squeezing, and actually causing Reagan to take a step closer rather than the step back as she wanted.

She looked up and met the eyes of the man. His hat was pulled low down on his head, probably so the wind wouldn't blow it away, and his coat hung loose over broad shoulders, unbuttoned. She didn't drag her eyes down, but she'd already noticed the jeans and boots.

She supposed they would draw the eye of a typical girl. And she had been a typical girl, earlier this year.

She wasn't anymore; she had a baby to protect, and she needed to do a better job for her brother. So despite the almost magnetic pull the man had on her, she turned her head away. She wasn't interested. Not even a little.

Chapter Two

Andrew stood at the door, somehow disappointed that the girl in front of him had turned away.

Her eyes had been the color of warm sugar cookies, expressive and hypnotizing, and he found himself feeling like they were talking without saying a word. It was an odd sensation.

He didn't know her and had never seen her before, and it was probably fanciful thinking on his part, maybe brought on by the holiday season, or maybe just the last week or so of owning a dog had affected him.

He almost laughed at that thought.

Gladys had affected him all right. She was so anxious and needy he could barely leave her alone; in fact, he didn't if he could help it, to the point of even taking her into the restroom with him. She lay on the floor while he showered, her eyes never leaving him.

Interestingly, his dog was now cowering behind the girl's legs. Normally, if he were anywhere around, Gladys was glued to his side. It had been that way since he'd taken her home, like she'd instantly bonded with him.

The woman in front of him wore a bulky sweatshirt and loose

pants. It was impossible to see even a hint of shape, not that it mattered. It was her eyes that intrigued him, or maybe the expression in them. Vulnerable and anxious, somehow they reminded him a little of Gladys, which was ridiculous.

His dog pushed on the back of the lady's legs, and she stumbled toward him. He reached out a hand to catch her, her arm feeling thin through the material of her extra-large sweatshirt.

"Sorry about that," he said, waiting until she seemed to have caught her balance before he dropped his hand.

She turned the sugar-cookie eyes on him again and her lips parted. Before she could say anything, a burst of friendly laughter came from Doc Violet. He'd barely her noticed standing back by an exam room door in conversation with Heather Johnson. Actually, Heather Clark now, as she'd just married Kade Clark, son of one of the most influential families in Cowboy Crossing. Heather appeared to be trying to talk, even as she struggled to hold onto the leash of Dara, a part Newfoundland mix who was almost as big as Heather.

Andrew had been out at Kade's many times, and Dara was a real sweetheart, even if she was as big as a small pony.

"Look! Andrew and Reagan are standing under the mistletoe." Doc Violet didn't say any more, but she didn't need to.

Heather was a romantic, and the whole town knew it, regardless of the pony and the grunt she'd married—saying grunt in the most affectionate way possible, since Andrew considered Kade a great friend. "You know what that means. It'll be the first kiss of the season." Heather's eyes danced. "Ha! I don't even know if any other businesses have it up."

"We decorate early for Christmas around here, and I just put that up this morning," Doc Violet said as she glanced at the Christmas tree in the corner, strung with lights shaped like bones and laden with dog biscuit ornaments. Andrew had no idea where a person would find decorations like that, but figuring that out was the least of his worries right now.

He could back away and refuse to do what Doc Violet and

Heather had just suggested—what mistletoe tradition demanded—but he didn't want the woman in front of him to get the idea it was her.

Her eyes already seemed like they held more hurt and baggage than a woman as young as she deserved.

Of course he didn't want it to force attention on her that she didn't want.

Plus, she could be married.

He could kiss her cheek.

As though in answer to that issue, Doc Violet said, "I think the mistletoe tradition only demands kissing when the people caught under it are unmarried and available."

"And my goodness, Reagan, you couldn't be caught under there with a more available man," Heather said with a gentle smile in her voice, her fondness for Reagan, who must be the woman in front of him, evident in her voice.

Reagan. Different, but he liked it. It seemed to suit her.

Her hair was darker than her eyes and fell down past her shoulders. Probably the conversation around her had made the red pop on her cheeks.

Pretty.

Young.

He didn't go around guessing women's ages that often, but he'd be willing to bet she was ten years younger than he.

That made him even more determined to kiss her cheek.

She hadn't moved away, and already several awkward seconds had ticked by while he did nothing.

He lifted a brow when she met his eyes, and she didn't shake her head, so he decided she'd come to the same conclusion. It was better to just do a simple kiss, make it so it didn't mean anything, and appease the people watching.

He shrugged, gave a little what-can-I-do-about-it grin, and lowered his head, aiming for her left cheek.

Unfortunately Gladys, who'd been cowering behind the woman's legs and had already knocked her off balance once, either didn't like him moving toward the woman—maybe Gladys was protecting her? —or maybe she was jealous.

That was the more likely scenario in his mind later when he thought about it.

Whatever it was, Gladys moved suddenly, knocking the woman off balance again and causing her to gasp.

He reached out again to stop her but was unable to halt the downward trajectory of his head as he opened his mouth to tell his dog to knock it off.

Everything happened so quickly.

Somehow the kiss that he planned—the peck that he'd intended— turned into a kiss he hadn't. Their mouths met. Shock rocked between them before something else seemed to take over. She sighed and pressed against him, and he forgot about steadying her with his hands on her shoulders and wrapped them around her back instead, deepening the kiss and feeling her tremble beneath him.

His own heart shuddered and sparked, and his mind shut down, and the room seemed to disappear, and he forgot about his good intentions and the people watching and the mistletoe and even the dog and instead sank into the feelings of the thousand nights and countless lonely days all disappearing. New thoughts cracked and opened and ripped away his unconscious thought that there would never be anyone for him, and the idea that a dog was better than a woman got shoved out of the way, and he quit thinking and focused only on the feeling of passion exploding and something blooming and coming to life, precious and delicate, strong and magnetic.

He probably would've stood there and kissed her for a lot longer, but vaguely he heard clapping and what sounded like cheering.

Andrew opened his eyes and drew back, suddenly aware again of where he was, who he was with, and the audience they had.

Reagan looked up at him, her eyes wide, her cheeks deep red, her lips swollen, and the dazed expression on her face probably mirroring his own.

They stared at each other, breathing erratically.

They'd never even spoken, and yet they'd shared a kiss that was quite possibly the most beautiful thing that had ever happened to him.

Maybe that's the way his relationships should be. No talking. No interaction. Just kissing.

She wouldn't be able to tell him how he was too unemotional and didn't meet her needs, whatever her needs were.

How he wasn't good enough, and how the death of his friend had caused him to grow bitter and angry and focused on his work, and how his wife had felt unloved and shut out until she felt like she needed to go find someone who understood and showed her he loved her by spending time with her and doing all the romantic things that Andrew never did.

Reagan's face had begun to clear, and he could see those hints on her. Hints that he wouldn't be enough. Hints that his inability to have the pretty words, to say the pretty words, to do the pretty things, to give her what she wanted, to show her the deep emotions that he was afraid to let out, would make him not be enough for this woman, either.

No matter how good the kiss was.

He saw it all, and he knew he should say something, apologize, make a joke, tell her she was beautiful and when she kissed him she made him forget his own name.

No. Not that last.

He should say something. Maybe a nod to the fact that he hadn't meant to kiss her like that. If his dog hadn't run into her and caused her to lose her balance, his cheek might've touched hers, and he probably would've ended up kissing the air beside it, and he wouldn't be standing here now, knowing he never had the right words, never said the right thing, and never showed enough of what he was feeling.

"That was about the best mistletoe kiss I've ever witnessed. And I think Gladys had a big part in that. Fitting, since I'm a vet." Doc Violet had come over and put a hand on each of their backs.

Which made Andrew want to move back.

He could, since he didn't have his dog cowering behind his legs.

Reaching deep, he tried to find the humorous veneer that he used to cover the deeper, harder parts that he couldn't let anyone see since his buddy and climbing partner Shane had plunged to his death, leaving Preston and him still clutching the mountain and listening to the yell echo off the stone until it faded and finally stopped abruptly.

Preston had turned to alcohol to numb the pain.

Andrew hadn't gone there, because he'd had two little boys and a wife to think of.

He ended up losing them anyway.

"So glad I can provide you with some holiday entertainment, Doc. Hopefully you can provide me with some advice about my dog." He gave Violet a grin, surface only. It didn't reach his eyes, he was sure, but no one ever noticed.

He turned to the woman who had just turned his world upside down and held his hand out. "I'm Andrew. I have to say I've never introduced myself to anyone quite like that before."

The woman seemed to gather herself, and if his brisk and heartless words, surface-only words, not soul-deep words like she deserved, hurt her, her sugar-cookie eyes didn't let it show.

She took his hand with cool reserve, her bulky sweatshirt tenting as she held her arm out and took his hand with cool fingers. Her head tilted, almost regally, and her voice held a touch of frost as she said, "It was a first for me too. I'm Reagan."

He noted she didn't say it was nice to meet him or any other pleasantry. Maybe she was making sure that he understood that the kiss meant nothing to her, or that there was nothing between them, or whatever. It was a stiff arm, and he recognized it.

Her fingers, strong despite their seeming fragility, squeezed his before her hand dropped.

Again, her eyes seemed to say so much, and he had the odd sense that they were holding a wordless conversation, knowledge passing between them without the need to articulate sentences. It was an odd sensation, to be able to communicate with someone without opening his mouth.

Maybe a good sensation, since so often he had to shove down anything that wanted to come out, just in case the bad stuff came out along with the good.

There was so much bad.

"Okay." Violet brushed her hands down her white lab coat. "Well, Reagan, you can go ahead and get the information from Andrew about his dog. I believe she's here for shots and a checkup."

"That's right. And I'm going to see if I can get you to give me a little advice on some issues I'm having with her." Andrew did not let his eyes follow Reagan as she handed him his leash before she turned and walked around the corner and through the door and back to the other side of the counter, pulling out a chair and sitting down with a plop, almost like her legs collapsed underneath her.

"I will certainly be happy to do what I can for you," Doc Violet said. "As soon as Reagan's done with you, you can go ahead and bring her into exam room two. I'll be waiting." She gave him a friendly smile and said a few more words to Heather before Heather pulled Dara up from a sitting position and gave him a wave as she walked out the door.

Seeing Heather walk out had reminded him that he'd forgotten to bring the paper in that he'd made up to put on the bulletin board.

Once Gladys was done with her appointment, he'd walk it back in from the truck.

He'd made the decision to rent out two of the large bedrooms in his house, not necessarily because he needed the money, although he'd never turn that down, but because Uncle Ron, his dad's older brother who lived with him, had seemed to be lonely last winter when Andrew was working twelve- and twenty-four-hour shifts at the firehouse in Trumbull.

Maybe having a renter or two would alleviate some of the long dark evenings and keep Uncle Ron's spirits up.

Reagan asked him the typical questions in a very professional and brisk tone, her eyes not meeting his, and although she was not unfriendly, she definitely was not welcoming. Even if he had wanted to follow up on the kiss with perhaps the offer of a date, or at least a conversation about anything not having to do with his dog and her health, her attitude clearly communicated that she wasn't interested.

Just as well, since he knew his ex was right. He hadn't been the most emotionally available person to begin with, and Shane's death had ruined what little bit of that ability he had.

If she had any lingering effects from the kiss, it wasn't obvious from the businesslike way she handled the paperwork as she typed his answers into the computer and did her job with professionalism.

The kiss had been an experience he wouldn't mind repeating, a lot, but he could understand that she might not have been affected the same way. That was life sometimes. Not to mention it wouldn't be fair of him to pursue a relationship when he knew he was so bad at them.

It was probably just best for him to focus on his job, which was very satisfying and included helping people and occasionally saving lives, and on his boys, because they were the most important thing in the world to him. It wasn't their fault that he'd been so deeply scarred by the death of his friend. He didn't want them to suffer any more than they already had.

He left the clinic almost an hour later, with a clean bill of health for Gladys, an appointment in two weeks to have her booster shots, and what he hoped would be some helpful information on how to help Gladys with her anxiety issues and her destructive tendencies when she wasn't able to be right by his side.

And as he slipped back in the door and tacked his "Room For Rent" sign on the bulletin board, if he noticed that Reagan was no longer at her desk, and if he wondered where she was and what she was doing, and if his thoughts lingered a little longer on the accidental kiss they'd shared under the mistletoe, he wouldn't let it go any further than that.

Chapter Three

"Oh, look! Reagan," Dylan exclaimed from beside her as Reagan fingered the piece of paper in her hand with the address on it. "There's a garage...and a barn! Maybe there will be room for me to bring the dirt bike that Uncle Nick gave me."

"It doesn't work, Dylan. There's no point in bringing it with us," Reagan said absentmindedly as she eyed the big old house. It was the only house in sight, down a long drive, a big barn hunched behind it, a little scary and threatening in her opinion, but she wasn't used to being out in the country this far.

Living in Trumbull had been far enough out. This was way beyond her comfort zone.

But she'd considered it a godsend when she checked the board two days after that horrible, awful, amazing, earth-shattering kiss and seen that someone had tacked up rooms for rent. She was getting desperate, and when she'd called, the kindly old gentleman she'd spoken with had seemed sweet and nice and not threatening at all.

She looked around again. Not a house or another person in sight.

How did people live like this? How could they stand to be so isolated?

There would be no walking to the store. No walking to the post office. No walking anywhere except for down long stretches of deserted highway. And one had to navigate the driveway first.

It appealed to a part of her, the part that wasn't pregnant—the adventurous part of her—the one that had her running on the cross-country team in high school and had her saving money to go backpacking across Europe.

The backpacking trip had never panned out, mostly because of Dylan, but now, it probably never would, because she had another life to think about.

Squaring her shoulders, she pushed through the gate and headed up the walk. They were expected, and if the rooms were anywhere near what they were supposed to be, she would be renting them. The price was right, the location of just outside Cowboy Crossing was perfect, and this would be great for Dylan.

"If they let us have the rooms, I'll ask about the garage," she said as Dylan walked quietly beside her. As he'd grown, he'd gotten quieter and more thoughtful, although no less of a risk-taker. More actually.

She wasn't sure what to do about that. Or if there was anything she could do. She didn't recall how her older brothers had navigated through the teen years, but she supposed there was something in a boy that made him want to do dangerous things. Just like there was something in her that wanted to keep him from it.

If he could be kept interested in working on the dirt bike which didn't run, maybe he would not be tempted to do some of the more outlandish things he'd mentioned to her in passing.

She highly doubted he could get the dirt bike running, so she wasn't really concerned about him hurting himself on that.

"Thanks, Reagan. I really want to bring it. I know I can get it together, I was watching YouTube videos about it, and I think I know what I was doing wrong the last time when I put it all together but it wouldn't start. There's an O-ring I missed."

She was listening, really, but what he was saying wasn't making any sense to her. Maybe if she'd seen it, maybe if she had time to focus on it, but she was just trying to survive and not make any more major mistakes.

Every time she thought about a mistake, she felt like she needed to put her hand over her stomach to assure the little one inside that she wasn't a mistake.

Reagan had made the mistake.

God didn't make mistakes.

She knew that. But God allowed her to face the consequences of her own bad choices.

Still, a person was never a mistake.

She knew that too. And that's why she always felt the need to remind her baby she was wanted, even if Reagan regretted the actions that created her.

Of course when she was thinking about mistakes, her most recent one—the kiss under the mistletoe—came to mind.

Not because it had been so wrong, necessarily, but more because it put thoughts in her head that were completely impossible, thoughts about men and dating and happily ever afters, and all those things that were no longer possible for her. At least not now, since she had her baby to think about.

Maybe there were men out there who would be interested in dating a woman who was carrying another man's child, but she'd never met any.

She didn't want to do that anyway. Her whole focus and being right now had to be on creating a stable home for her brother and her child.

That kiss had distracted her from everything she knew she needed to be doing.

It was a mistake.

And there she was, thinking about it again.

At least she was thinking about the kiss now, and not the man who had given it to her.

Dylan walked beside her as they stepped up the porch steps and onto the big wide country porch where a swing hung at one end and comfortable-looking rocking chairs sat on the other. Inviting, and it made her hope the rooms would be just as perfect.

She knocked on the large wooden door.

A cool breeze rustled the leaves of the oak tree in the yard. Many leaves had not fallen yet and were pulled off with the tug of the air and fluttered onto the porch.

Watching the leaves gave Reagan the oddest desire to just float. No more struggling, no more striving, no more hurt or pain. Just floating.

It seemed so unfair that some people's lives just seemed to be floating lives, with no real problems or issues, while her life had seemed to be one long fight and struggle.

A struggle to survive, a struggle to see her parents stay together, a struggle to see her mother leave, a struggle to see her father sink into the bottle and prison before leaving his family, chasing the promise of a good time in a woman's arms, and when that didn't pan out, he found someone else and someone else and had never made it back home.

A struggle to watch her brothers leave and assure them it was okay, that she could raise Dylan and take care of herself too. Even though she was only eighteen.

She'd been wrong. Obviously. Since it hadn't been but a few years later when she'd been seduced by the pretty words of a professional man, who'd promised her that she was beautiful and desirable and everything he ever wanted and he was leaving his wife for her.

It'd only taken him one night, not even all night, just the date and what came after, for him to decide that he wasn't leaving his wife after all.

In hindsight, Reagan could see nothing he'd said had been true, and she'd believed every lie.

Struggle. That had only increased it.

She sighed and turned back to the door, rapping again, as Dylan shifted beside her.

"I like this place, Reagan. I hope we get it," he said softly beside her.

As much as it scared her to be so far away from any other people, there was definitely something homey about this place.

And if the man who was renting the room was as kindly and grandfatherly as he sounded, then maybe they would feel at home. She was eager to meet him.

Maybe that's why there was a smile on her face as the door opened and a man came into view.

Only he wasn't old, and he wasn't grandfatherly, and he wasn't someone she wanted to see.

Her stomach lurched and shook, not that sturdy in the best of times in her current condition, and as it dipped and swayed, she put a hand over her bulky sweatshirt, pressing in, knowing she wouldn't throw up, but the feeling was there.

The man. The man she couldn't stop thinking about, the one that had derailed her from her purpose and made her think things that were impossible for a woman facing the situation she was facing. Making her long for the little girl dreams that she'd left behind and wish she were free to find out who he was and if he might be interested in the same things she was.

The man she'd vowed to stay away from and stop thinking about.

His eyes had widened. His mouth, maybe open to form some kind of greeting, didn't move. The strong nose and jaw she couldn't forget were in stark relief behind the screen of the storm door. She couldn't see the dark swirl of his irises, but it wasn't hard for her to remember the stone gray with just a touch of brown. Eyes she could get lost in.

She knew the danger and lifted her chin. "I'm here to see Mr.

Ron. We spoke on the phone about the rooms he has for rent. He's expecting me."

Apparently this man, Andrew—she remembered his name—apparently he rented rooms here too.

This was the only place she knew of, in Cowboy Crossing and the surrounding areas, that was renting rooms she could afford. But she didn't want to be stuck in the same house with him. He hadn't even opened the screen door, hadn't touched her, she couldn't even see his eyes that well, and her heart was racing, her breath had shortened.

Whatever it was about him, it was dangerous for her to be around him. She was tempted to make the same mistake that she'd already made; she hadn't been this attracted to Dr. Michael.

The man cleared his throat and pushed open the door. "Ron's my uncle. He lives here with me, and he told me you were coming." He seemed to catch himself. "Not you, someone. He told me someone was coming." His eyes slanted to Dylan. "He said you'd be bringing your brother with you." He held out his hand to Dylan. "I'm Andrew."

Reagan almost smiled as Dylan's eyes popped open, and he looked from Andrew's hand to Andrew and back again before lifting his own hand and clasping it.

It wasn't that the kid wasn't used to men, because he had two older brothers in their twenties, but typically his brothers didn't shake his hand.

Reagan appreciated it.

"I'm Dylan." His eyes slid to Reagan before they went back to Andrew. "It's nice to meet you."

Reagan made a note to tell Dylan later that he did a great job.

Andrew jerked his head, and if he was embarrassed about the kiss they shared or had any thoughts about it, she couldn't tell by looking at him. "I remember your name is Reagan. In case you forgot mine, it's Andrew."

"I remember," she said. "Gladys too. She was a sweetheart."

"Yeah. Violet gave me some tips for her, they worked a little, I guess. She, um, doesn't like to be separated from me." His brows crumpled just a little. "Although she seemed to like you okay. Which is weird, because you're the first person I've seen her do that with."

Maybe, if Reagan felt free to flirt, she would bat her eyes a little and ask him what exactly he meant by "that." Implying "that" meant Gladys had shoved them together for a kiss.

But even before she'd made her mistake, she hadn't been a flirty kind of girl. She definitely loved to have fun, and she'd loved being active—climbing the trails in the hills around their home, running and cycling, and even taking the occasional whitewater rafting trip, compliments of a friend who was a guide down the river in the Ozarks. But she'd never been a flirt.

"Maybe she could just tell that I liked her."

Andrew's eyes flickered, but his shoulder lifted. "Maybe."

He opened the door wider and stepped back, one hand holding the screen door open. "Come on in. I'll show you the rooms that are for rent."

Dylan waited for her to walk in first, and she tried to ignore Andrew's nearness as she slid by him and into the grand foyer of the house.

"It's gorgeous in here," she said, without really thinking. Just saying the thoughts in her head. Old woodwork, wide stairs, hardwood floor that was obviously old and worn, though well cared for. The house had character, and she loved it instantly, surprisingly, or maybe not so much, since she'd never lived anywhere so grand. It was a far cry from the two-bedroom apartment she was renting in Trumbull.

"Thank you. It's been in my family for generations. My sisters weren't interested in it, and so I came back and paid for their shares when my parents died."

"Is this a real ranch?" Dylan asked.

Dylan had been growing quieter and quieter over the last year, but before that, he had been predisposed to ramble on and on. Reagan hoped he didn't have a relapse. For some reason, she wanted to see Dylan and Andrew get along.

"It is. But I've been renting out most of the ground. I'm the fire chief in Trumbull, and I work twenty-four-hour shifts, plus I volunteer at the fire station in Cowboy Crossing, and it takes a lot of time. My parents were renting the acreage before I bought it. I just left things the way they were."

Dylan had asked the question, and Andrew started out speaking to him, but by the time he was done, his gaze had traveled to Reagan, and he seemed to be watching her.

She wasn't sure why. Unless he was telling her he didn't want someone in her condition bringing a baby into his home. But that was kind of presumptuous, since she hadn't told him, asked him, or even suggested it, and from what she'd been told by the people that she'd been around, they didn't even know she was pregnant until she told them. They just assumed she was pleasantly plump and wore big clothes.

Maybe that was a result of her natural slenderness, because the midwife had assured her that her baby was measuring the proper size. The midwife had also said something about her stomach muscles and first babies, and people who were as fit as she was, but she hadn't really been paying attention at the time, because she had still been trying to wrap her head around the changes in her life and body.

Her pregnancy was no better a subject than the kiss. Dylan had no idea, and maybe a flash of panic crossed her face, because his eyebrows shifted before he seemed to shake his head and look away.

"How about I show you the rooms first, then we'll come back down and I'll show you the kitchen and the living room. Basically, I was thinking that whoever rented the rooms would have access to the kitchen and the whole downstairs, assuming, of course, you clean up after yourself. This isn't a bed-and-breakfast." He didn't say the last lines unkindly but almost as though it was something he hadn't thought of. "I'm sorry, this is the first time I've rented any rooms out, and I guess I'm just kind of establishing the ground rules in my head."

Why decide to rent now?

As though he had anticipated her unspoken question, he said, "You spoke with my uncle Ron. I know last winter it was just him and me in this big old house, and when I'm working some of my longer shifts or get called out on accident, I know it gets lonely here for him by himself. The idea was that I would rent rooms, and he would have company."

"Where is he now?" Dylan asked, following Reagan up the steps.

"He usually takes a nap in the afternoon. He's sleeping on the recliner in the living room." Andrew reached the top of the stairs and turned around with a little smile. "It probably will upset him that I didn't wake him up. But his afternoon nap is like clockwork."

Reagan found herself smiling, and some of her discomfort faded. She hadn't wanted to be stuck in the same house as the person she'd shared such a passionate mistletoe kiss with, especially since she wasn't interested in any kind of relationship, but maybe things wouldn't be as awkward as she'd thought they might be. At least he didn't seem to be inclined to pursue anything beyond casual friendliness. Which suited her exactly.

"The two rooms you're sharing are joining, and one is slightly smaller than the other. I think they might have originally been intended to be a master bedroom and a nursery or possibly a bedroom and a sitting room together."

He shrugged, a casual motion that drew Reagan's eye. "Regardless, they both have beds and dressers in them, but no bathrooms. There's just one of those upstairs, and that's here." He pointed to the door at the end of the hall. "There's a half bath downstairs, but this is the only shower. I work odd hours, so it isn't going to be a big deal about splitting shower time." He eyed Reagan, that grin still turning his lips up. "I have older sisters, and I understand that ladies in the shower can take a while. That's just something you and your brother can hash out."

"What about Uncle Ron?" Dylan asked.

Andrew gave a half chuckle, half grunt. "He showers, but I wouldn't say it's regularly."

Reagan wanted to look away, because it was so endearing the way one side of his mouth lifted up higher than the other in that lopsided grin. Dylan didn't seem to understand what he was saying, but when his eyes shifted to her again, she had to grin back.

She liked him in spite of herself, and that probably wasn't good, but it definitely made her feel more relaxed. Obviously, Dylan liked him too. He almost had that hero worship look in his eyes that he had with his older brothers when they were around. He would've gone with them in a heartbeat if Reagan had let him.

Maybe she should have.

Andrew opened the bathroom door, and Dylan peered in with interest, while Reagan was slightly more reserved. A shower-tub combo, a sink, and a toilet. A couple of towel racks and a rug on the floor. Nothing fancy, and none of the warm touches a woman might have made to make things look homier.

The hall had been the same. No pictures, no flowers, nothing to warm the cold white walls.

There weren't even any curtains in the windows.

Andrew led them to the bedrooms, and they were just as classic and just as plain. White walls, a dresser, and a bed with a nondescript comforter.

They were serviceable, and they looked clean.

"I have a housekeeper that comes in once a week and cleans. If you don't want her in your bedroom, just say so. There's a sweeper downstairs in the closet. You'll have to carry it up to sweep up here."

He was all business, which was probably how it should be. Although Reagan kind of missed the smile and the shared joke. Maybe rather than relaxing him, it had scared him.

She should probably feel relief. He didn't seem to want to relive that kiss or bring it out into the open any more than she did.

She felt their secret was safe.

Going downstairs, he showed them the kitchen, and they peeked in the living room where, sure enough, Uncle Ron was leaned back in his recliner, his mouth open and his mustache wiggling with every snore.

It was endearing in an elderly gentleman kind of way, and it made Reagan automatically like the old man, as she had when she spoke with him on the phone.

"And that's pretty much it. Like I said, the kitchen is yours, you cook for yourself, and I'll give you space in the refrigerator to keep your groceries." He paused here, almost as though he was thinking, and then he said, "If you want to make regular meals and feed Uncle Ron every day, and me when I'm here, I'll take some money off the rent. And I'll buy the groceries."

Reagan considered that. It would be nice to have a little less to pay, but would she be able to keep it up when the baby came?

She decided to chance it. "I'll take you up on it."

He named a figure that felt fair to her, and she agreed to it.

"Does this mean you're interested in the rooms?" he asked.

"I am. How soon can we move in?" It wasn't even that she had any choice. If she didn't take these, she wasn't sure exactly what they were going to do. Thankfully these suited in every way.

"Well, you saw them, they're ready. Whatever works for you."

"There's a week left until the end of the month when we need to move out of our apartment. How about we'll start moving things in, although there really isn't much to move." She considered putting her bed in storage, because she owned it, but she'd bought it secondhand, and actually, Dylan's daybed that he slept in had been in the apartment when they moved in.

"If you need some help, I can give you a hand." His words were casual, but when she looked at his face, it seemed like he was surprised that he had spoken.

"That shouldn't be necessary. But thank you. Let me give you a check." She reached for the shoulder strap of her purse and slid it off her shoulder.

Andrew shifted, like the idea made him uncomfortable, but he didn't say anything. She pulled her checkbook out.

"Do you want a security deposit as well?" she asked, hoping that he would say no. She wasn't sure she had enough in her account to cover the first month's rent along with a security deposit. Not until she got paid on Friday. That was four days away.

"No. I don't."

She almost thought that maybe he was making that up as he answered and hadn't actually planned on whether or not a security deposit would be necessary.

He said this was his first time renting. She definitely believed it.

Still, relief was cool and sharp in her chest. She hadn't wanted to admit how low her funds were and how close to the edge she lived, paycheck to paycheck.

She didn't want to get into her past and her home situation, although surely he would wonder just a little bit why she was running around with her brother in tow.

Maybe he didn't care. He seemed like the kind of man who had other things to think about than her personal history.

Thankfully.

She tore the check out and handed it to him. "I assume the rent will be due on the first of every month?"

He nodded. "That's what I was just going to say. I know we're a few days early, right now, but let's just plan on that. You guys can move in anytime, and we'll use the first as our due date. That'll keep things simple."

She could appreciate that. "Thank you."

He reached out to take the check, and their fingers brushed. She hadn't been prepared for that, but she didn't allow anything that she felt show on her face. In fact, she turned away immediately.

"Thank you so much for your time." She didn't need to tell Dylan to come; he opened the door for her.

She realized as they walked out what bothered her more than anything. Well, more than anything except the fact there was what amounted to a secret history between them. It was the drab nature of the house. She should have asked if she could throw some decorations up. She wasn't sure she wanted to live somewhere that was so depressing.

She didn't think he'd mind. But she'd be sure to ask the next time she saw him.

Chapter Four

"I thought you said you wanted to rent to a man?" Preston huffed as his biceps curled and the weight came up.

Andrew lifted his own weight and wished he hadn't started the conversation. He'd rather concentrate on counting his sets and reps than think about his new renter and her brother.

Not that he'd been able to think about anything else all day.

"I wasn't the one who told her to come look at the rooms. Uncle Ron had. When she showed up at the door, I wanted to tell her that I had someone else and I'd let her know, but I just couldn't lie."

They hit their ten reps and set the weights down for a rest.

"Is she cute?" Preston smirked, his bloodshot eyes narrowing slightly. Ladies had always considered Preston good-looking and easy to talk to, but the death of Shane had affected him too.

All three of them had been on that rock wall. Only two of them had survived.

No doubt the experience had brought Preston and Andrew closer, but there was always that elephant between them, because they certainly didn't talk about that day. Nor of Shane.

Both of them were handling things differently.

Preston had turned to drink, which, thankfully, was one vice Andrew didn't have. Although they'd both lost their marriages over the accident.

"I guess she is. She had on a baggy sweatshirt and a big scarf, and I don't even remember what else she was wearing, because I wasn't paying attention. I don't want to be attracted to my renter. There are probably laws against that or something."

Andrew didn't have any idea. He should look up the renting laws, but it had been a spur-of-the-moment thing. He hadn't expected to put his ad up and get a renter within a week. He'd thought it was going to take a little longer.

"I don't think so. You're not her employer or anything." Preston wiped his forehead with the towel around his neck, then wrapped his hands around his weights to begin the second set of reps.

Andrew didn't need a towel, he'd never been a sweater, but he followed Preston's lead and started his second set as well.

"Did you hear anything about your new job?" Preston asked when he finished the second set of reps and laid his weight down.

"Nah. It's kinda soon. And I'm honestly not sure what I'm going to do if I'm hired there anyway."

When Andrew had seen the ad for a first responder instructor, he applied online, thinking that it might be better hours, if not better pay, than the fire chief position. Not to mention the job was in Cowboy Crossing rather than Trumbull.

The main reason he wanted a change of pace was Uncle Ron. Andrew felt like he spent an awful lot of time away from home, and the old man was lonely. Plus, if the new job worked out, he might be able to start ranching on his own rather than renting his ground out.

All thoughts and ideas for down the road. He didn't really want to give up his fire chief position.

He eyed his friend, who was wiping his forehead again with his towel. It was guy code to not talk about personal stuff, but he didn't feel like he was being a very good friend if he didn't mention it. "You gonna lay off the drink?"

Not even a flicker of annoyance crossed Preston's face. In fact, he grinned. "I don't see any reason why I should."

"Killing ya, man." He wasn't even joking about that. Preston looked sallow and skinny, and his butt was dragging.

"Gonna die sometime. Better early than late. I'll have more people at my funeral." He gave the devil-may-care grin, the one that always got him a date in high school. It was probably what had attracted Tiffany, his ex-wife, to him as well.

"But then the rest of us have to live without you. It's kind of inconsiderate." That was the closest either one of them ever got to talking about Shane, and them surviving when he didn't.

Andrew could keep from making any more human connections; he had been really good at focusing on his job and saving people, then walking away. He'd walked away from his marriage. But he couldn't keep himself from caring about his friend.

Caring about people meant pain, and he preferred to not care about anyone.

"You can grab a six pack and join me in front of the TV tonight. No one's stopping you." Preston jerked his head up, then grabbed his weights for the last set.

"You know I'll pass. I don't need another vice." Andrew grabbed his own weights and started his last set as well.

They lifted in silence for a bit. Even though their conversation hadn't been exactly friendly, their silence was the easy silence of old friends.

As Preston laid his weights down after finishing the rep, he said, "You know, you could invite me to Thanksgiving. That's the least you could do, if you're really concerned about my health and welfare."

"Thought you'd be going down to Mommy and Daddy and the big family celebration in Dallas. I can't imagine they'd want their boy Preston to be anywhere else for Thanksgiving."

"Which is exactly why I'm not going to be there. Invite me, man, so I have an excuse when Mom calls."

"You know you're always welcome. It's just going to be Uncle Ron and me." Andrew didn't add that maybe his renter would be there too. Unless she had family she was going to spend the holidays with.

Preston gave him a sideways glance as he wiped his forehead with his towel. "What about Athena?" His tone was casual. Too casual to Andrew's ears, but Andrew didn't say anything.

Athena wouldn't have anything to do with Preston. Preston might've had a crush on her for years, but he wouldn't do anything either. He knew he wasn't good enough for her.

"I don't know. I guess I'll be calling her or, more likely, she'll call me." His oldest sister had always been bossy and sure of what she wanted. "It probably depends on what her assignment is and what she's doing."

She hired out as a private nurse and made good money doing it. But it also meant that she typically didn't have holidays and weekends off like most people which suited Athena just fine.

"Well, this is going to be the year she notices me, so make sure she's there." Preston gave Andrew a smile that didn't even begin to reach his eyes and stepped away from the bench. "You coming?"

Andrew realized he was just sitting there. He stood. "My boys will be there too, unless my ex screws me out of another holiday. I wouldn't put it past her."

They walked to the locker room together, and Preston laughed. "Some kind of baloney about the boys needing to know what real holidays and families are and you can't provide that for them and she wants them to have the memories of Norman Rockwell beauty to take into adulthood with them?" Preston had just the right amount of snob in his voice.

Andrew shouldn't laugh, because he was totally making fun of Cheyenne, but he'd paraphrased her arguments so well he couldn't help it.

"Yeah. You know it."

"Well, maybe the boys would like to have a few memories of

holidays with their dad," Preston said, and the bitterness was undisguised in his voice.

Preston hadn't had a dad growing up, and he was a little sensitive about the topic.

Andrew had three older sisters, but Athena was the only one that would want to spend the holiday with him and Uncle Ron. Their family hadn't exactly been close growing up. Not that he didn't love his other two sisters, they just weren't real interested in coming back to the heartland for the holidays.

By the time Preston and he were changed and walking out, they were talking about the accident that had taken place on I-66, and Andrew was telling him what he knew about it. As a fire chief in Trumbull and as part of the volunteer fire company in Cowboy Crossing, he had the inside scoop on any accidents.

His fire chief job was also the reason he was at the gym. He wanted to be prepared physically for anything that he might be asked to do.

It was understandable that Preston, as a whitewater rafting tour adventure guide in the Ozarks just to the south, wanted to stay in shape too. It was natural for them to be gym buddies.

Andrew pushed out the front door and was just getting ready to call goodbye to Preston, who was parked in the opposite direction, when his eyes hooked on a figure struggling in the doorway right beside the gym.

He assumed the doorway led to apartments either above the gym or the building beside, and it looked like the person was moving out.

His eyes recognized her immediately, although it took his brain a couple of seconds to catch up as he took in the scene and the girl struggling to move what looked like a wooden chest out of the tight doorway, her baggy clothes hanging off her, and a voice—Andrew assumed it was her brother—calling from the interior where the other half of the chest had not emerged. It seemed to be caught on something.

She didn't notice him at first but looked up as he walked over. He felt Preston's presence behind him, and Preston was probably thinking the same thing he was about giving them a hand, although he would have no idea that Andrew knew this girl.

Why couldn't he look at her without thinking about that kiss?

Preston definitely didn't need to know about that.

The fading light emphasized the sparkly lights of the candy cane decorations on the pole above them, and the Christmas music the gym had been playing hummed softly through the closed door as he stopped beside Reagan.

"I told you I would help you. You should have called."

She gasped and straightened and then stepped back. A little off balance, probably because she had been pulling so hard on the chest.

"I couldn't have done that. Dylan and I can get it." Her voice was still that husky smoothness he remembered, and it stirred in his chest like soft leather wrapping around his heart. He ignored the feeling.

Preston snickered behind him, covering it with a cough, but Andrew wasn't fooled.

He didn't know why Preston would be snickering. The girl wasn't gorgeous. She certainly dressed like a hobo with more baggy clothes and her hair thrown up in some kind of haphazard half-bun half-ponytail hybrid thing.

Preston had known him for a long time and apparently didn't even have to see his face to know that this girl could be different.

Not that Andrew would allow her to be.

"Well, my buddy and I are here now. We'll give you guys a hand." It was odd, but Andrew just stood there, looking at her. Normally he didn't stand around waiting. But for some reason, she kind of froze him and just made him want to watch her. Which was odd.

The spell didn't last long, because Preston broke in. "Why, Andrew. How kind of you to ask me if I would like to help this young lady. I'm so glad you thought of me, and I'm honored to be asked. Of course I'll help you." Preston was in full-on smart-aleck mode and even bowed in Reagan's general direction with a silly grin that had her smiling back at him.

Their silly by-play sent a pang through Andrew along with a shaft of irritation.

Why was Preston even bothering to try to charm her? He wasn't going to do anything more than move her chest and leave.

Neither was Andrew.

That didn't mean he couldn't be nice while he was here.

Irritation at himself warred with the irritation at his friend, because of his own stupid reaction. Reagan could laugh and smile with whoever she wanted to laugh and smile with, and it didn't mean a thing to Andrew.

"A lady in your condition shouldn't be lifting heavy things like this anyway. As my friend just said, you should ask him to help you." Preston bowed again. "Allow us. And where are you taking it?"

A lady in her condition? What in the world?

Reagan turned and pointed to the blue car three spaces up, with the hatch up. "I think it'll fit in there. It seems like it would anyway."

Andrew looked dubiously at the car. But he didn't say anything.

"Andrew has a pickup, we can put it in the back of that, and he can take it wherever you want to go."

"This is the renter I was telling you about," Andrew said. "Reagan, this is my friend Preston. I just invited him for Thanksgiving dinner, so if you're planning on eating at the house, which I know we haven't talked about, he'll be there. Preston, this is Reagan." He turned, indicating the doorway that was blocked by the chest that was still half in and half out of it. "And that's her brother, Dylan."

"I can get this end. I'm strong. Reagan was having trouble with her side. It's stuck somehow," Dylan said rather than returning the introduction.

Andrew would have expected Preston to give the kid a hard time, but he didn't.

"The renter." Preston's voice still held that annoying teasing note as he stood with his hands on his hips looking between Andrew and Reagan. "Believe it or not, we were just talking about you." He nodded his head, his whole body moving up and down. The way he was talking about her made it sound like they had been spending hours discussing her entire life history rather than a few sentences at most.

"I told him I had a renter. That was the extent of our conversation about you." Andrew's words came out short. He didn't want Reagan to think that he was talking about kissing her under the mistletoe.

Or anything else. Any weird interest.

Even if he had a weird interest. He wasn't talking about it.

Reagan jerked her chin at him, her friendly smile fading which annoyed Andrew even more. They had a little tenuous thread of shared humor between them before she had left his house, and he wished he could get that back. Now he felt like there were chasms between them with Preston standing there smirking at him.

"Come on, old man," Preston said. "Let's get this out of the doorway for the lady in distress. Then you can go get your truck and take this to your house." Preston peeked in the doorway. "I think the brother can give you a hand getting the chest in the house when you get there." He gave him an eyeball. "I can't believe you'd allow a lady in her condition move furniture around. What kind of fire chief and EMT are you anyway?" He smirked. Like his previous smirks, this one had not reached his eyes, either. "Maybe you're trying to drum up work? Or maybe you're just trying to make the news."

What in the world was Preston talking about? Andrew scratched his head and met Preston's gaze, but he didn't say anything and ended up just rolling his eyes and shaking his head and turning back to the chest.

After examining it, he said, "I think it's caught down here on a nail sticking up from the doorjamb. I think if we lifted it up an inch, we'll be able to get it over that hump and get it out of the doorway."

He looked at Reagan, his face carefully expressionless. "Is that okay with you? If we put this in the back of my pickup? Dylan and I can get it out and carry it upstairs to your room when we get there."

She nodded, biting one lip which somehow made her seem vulnerable and young. And it made him want to protect and shield her from the harsh realities of life. Whatever had happened in her life that had left her in charge of her younger brother and trying to make a living on her own.

It also reminded him of mistletoe.

He tore his eyes away and looked over the buildings lining the street, the Christmas decorations that already blinked even though it wasn't even Thanksgiving yet, and the traffic signal that was just now turning from yellow to red. Anything to keep from looking at her, and her lips, and thinking about mistletoe.

"If it's not too much trouble, I guess that's what we need to do. I'm sorry to put you out." That voice was soft and smooth like wheat kernels through his fingers—a childhood memory he hadn't thought of in years, but being around Reagan and that voice, or maybe it was the holiday season, one couldn't help but think about family and good memories.

"You're not putting me out at all. I'm expecting Dylan to do most of the work anyway." Andrew caught the eye of the boy in the stairwell, and his grin split his face wide open.

"I can do it," the boy said eagerly.

Andrew could totally commiserate. Growing up with three older sisters, he'd always wanted to prove that he could do things too.

That seemed like a long time ago. But Dylan also reminded him so much of his own boys. Maybe his boys were just a little older, but it was such a great age, and they had so much fun together.

Those thoughts sent longing through him.

He didn't miss Cheyenne. He didn't hate her or anything, just didn't have any particular special feelings for her. Other than maybe a mild annoyance and a slight hurt that their marriage hadn't worked out.

They'd decided they wanted different things and agreed to

divorce. But sometimes he wished they'd held it together for their boys. It killed him to not get to spend time with them like he wanted to.

After growing up with three older sisters, he'd been thrilled to have two boys of his own.

He hadn't expected Cheyenne to move to Chicago when she left.

Shaking those thoughts away, he said, "I guess that settles it then."

He reached down, and after a little bit of struggle, they were able to get the hope chest over the nail on the doorjamb and out the doorway. It sat on the sidewalk while he went around to the back lot and grabbed his pickup.

When he came back, Preston was saying something and gesturing with his arms, and Reagan was laughing, not smiling, not grinning, but belly laughing. Dylan laughed along with her.

He didn't hate his friend, but he kind of resented him at that point.

He wanted to be the one to make Reagan laugh. Which was stupid. And he recognized the feeling immediately as stupidity, but that didn't change it.

"And there she was, police cars all around her vehicle, and the firefighter that she babysat when she was a teenager stuck in the front seat of her car, delivering her baby. They shut down all six lanes of the Beltway outside of Dallas for an hour during rush hour. It was nuts. But the baby was healthy, and they named him Dax after the guy who delivered him. When they ran the story in the paper, they had a picture of the woman when she was babysitting him. Pretty cool."

Andrew walked over in time to catch the end of that, and he wondered why in the world Preston was telling that story. He recognized the story, but it had happened over ten years ago, and yes, it was funny, but what had brought that up?

"All right. Looks like the hero's back. I'll grab this and toss it in the back of his pickup, then I'm outta here. Nice to meet you, Reagan."

"Nice to meet you too, Preston. We'll see you on Thanksgiving if not before." She gave him a sweet smile, her voice just as throaty and smooth as it had been before, and Andrew looked away, wishing he could close his ears too.

"Dylan and I have some things to bring down yet and put in the car. We'll be out in a bit to your place."

Andrew assumed she was talking to him, and he grudgingly turned his head back, jerking it in acknowledgment before going to the chest and lifting it with Preston.

The two of them disappeared up the stairs and into the building.

"You didn't tell me your renter was pregnant," Preston said immediately when they were gone.

The chest slipped out of his hand, the corner of it smacking his toe, which wouldn't have hurt at all if he'd had his work boots on. But since he was wearing sneakers, it cut short and hard, and he figured his toenail would be black, and he'd be lucky if he didn't lose it.

His leg throbbed, his foot and toe feeling like they were as big as tree trunks, and he bent over the chest. But he looked up, one eye squinted, his head tilted.

"Pregnant?"

"Can't you tell with her stomach sticking out like a basketball? I didn't ask when she was due, but I'd guess soon." Preston grunted as he set his end of the chest down. "We gonna move this thing today, or are you gonna stand there and think about levitation?"

"You asked her if she was pregnant?" Andrew's stomach still hadn't settled. It was rolling around like marbles in a jar, and his head was kind of spinning. The pain in his toe wasn't helping his concentration, either.

"I didn't have to ask her. I could tell she was."

Preston had to be wrong. Andrew tried to remember what she looked like, but the baggy clothes had hidden her figure.

"I said she is lucky to be living with you, an EMT and a

firefighter, and she agreed that if she didn't make it to the hospital in time you could deliver her baby, and then I launched into the story about the firefighter who delivered the baby." Preston crossed his arms over his chest. "I guess I shouldn't expect you to notice. But I honestly can't figure out how you could miss it."

He had. He'd totally missed it. But now that he was thinking about it, it made sense. And he actually remembered seeing her put her hand on her stomach yesterday when they were walking through his house. He hadn't thought too much of it at the time, because he'd been more interested in her lips and thinking about mistletoe.

Stupid.

So was she moving out of her boyfriend's house? Where was the father?

This should make him less interested in her, but for some reason, it made him more. And opened up a whole list of questions he wanted answered. It couldn't be natural to be this interested in his renter.

Of course, it wasn't exactly natural to have the person, the stranger, that he had shared the most passionate kiss of his life with, renting rooms from him.

This entire time, he thought it was nothing but stupid, and nothing had happened today that had changed his mind.

Although at this point, the idea of not having her in his house kind of made him itchy.

"Thanks. I need to get home. I've got Gladys in her cage, and she hates it."

"Tell me again why you named your dog Gladys?"

He ignored the question, not wanting to explain that she'd had that name when he'd adopted her and he'd been too slow in changing it.

Gladys had stuck.

Chapter Five

Reagan set the bag of hamster bedding on the counter at the feed store.

Marlowe Hudson smiled at her and scanned it. "It's good to see you, Reagan. How are you feeling, and how's the baby doing?"

Reagan nodded. "She's doing fine. The midwife says she's growing perfectly and everything's good."

"Your due date's coming up. The day before Christmas, right?" Marlowe asked as she grabbed the bag and put the litter in it.

"That's right. Christmas Eve. Poor planning, wasn't it?"

Zero planning. That's what it was. Her joke was weak at best.

"I think if Christmas is a good enough day for Jesus to be born, it's good enough for anyone else. Maybe you'll be a day late."

"That would hardly be fair for the baby. Christmas and her birthday on the same day."

"True, I guess. Still, I think that would be sweet. What a way to celebrate Christmas." Marlowe took the debit card that Reagan handed her and swiped it across the slot on the cash register. "Grandma Hudson is having a big Thanksgiving dinner at her house.

I'm sure you're welcome if you want to come," she said casually, with no mention of the fact that Reagan's family wasn't the greatest. "Dylan and your older brothers are welcome as well. Maybe you guys already have something planned together?"

"No. Nothing planned. But I am renting rooms now, and I might cook Thanksgiving dinner for everyone there." They hadn't talked about it, but she'd agreed to make meals in return for having her rent reduced. "How is Mrs. Hudson handling things?"

"Don't overdo it," Marlowe said as she handed Reagan's debit card back. "That's a lot to take on, and you should be taking it easy with working full time and now moving." Marlowe gave a smile. "You know I just have your best interest at heart. Sorry. I'm a little bossy at times. Mrs. Hudson is doing well. It was a shock to everyone, the news about Mr. Hudson, but I've never seen anyone handle things with such grace and faith. All the advice she's handed out over the years seems to come from an internal well that she actually lives by. She's doing fine."

"I'm glad to hear it. And don't worry about being bossy. Sometimes I need someone to give me the knowledge in order for me to do what I know I should."

"We all do sometimes." Marlowe seemed to be thinking about something, as her eyes clouded over for just a bit. Then she shook herself. "Who are you renting from? Where at? I didn't even know there were places available. Is it in Cowboy Crossing?"

Reagan tried to keep up with all the questions Marlowe lobbed at her. "Yes. From Andrew Coleman. You know he's the fire chief in Trumbull, but he volunteers here. He's renting rooms in his farmhouse just outside of town. A beautiful house. I love it. And I hope he'll let me do some decorating."

Marlowe's eyes had gotten big. "Andrew?" A grin tugged her mouth up, and she leaned over the counter. "Andrew Coleman is gorgeous. And he needs a wife."

"I heard that, Marlowe," a voice called from the far corner of the store where Clark, Marlowe's husband, was hanging Christmas decorations from the ceiling.

"You heard nothing, Gable," Marlowe called back with a smirk and a much louder voice. Then, in the same conspiratorial tone she'd used earlier, she said, "I'm serious. He's such a great guy, and he's amazing with his boys, and he's always ready to lend a hand to anyone. I'd love to see him get a good wife. I don't even think he knows he needs it. Maybe with you living under the same roof, you'll open his eyes."

"He'll open his eyes and see a pregnant woman who will soon have a baby and has a brother that she takes everywhere with her, too." Reagan pulled a lip back and looked at Marlowe under her brows. "There's nothing desirable in that."

"Andrew really isn't like other guys. I don't think any of that would mean anything to him. I do think he used to do some kind of extreme sports, but I'm not sure exactly what. There was some kind of tragedy, and he gave everything up." Marlowe tapped a finger on her chin. "But sometimes it's hard for guys like that to settle down. I don't know if that had anything to do with his divorce or not. That's all gossip. Regardless, my point is don't discount it. He's a good man."

"Well, I'm renting from him because I have to, but I certainly don't have any ideas like that in my head." She did have ideas about the kiss they'd shared. That was definitely in her head. They hadn't made their way to her heart though, and she didn't intend for them to. Wouldn't allow that.

Although it had been kind of him to help her with her chest. By the time she got home and out of her car, he'd already grabbed Dylan and had him help carry it upstairs and put it in the bigger of the two rooms.

She supposed she'd need the bigger room, since she'd have a baby in hers soon.

She grabbed her bag. "Thanks, Marlowe. I hope you have a great Thanksgiving. And tell Mrs. Hudson and Mr. Hudson I asked about them." She almost said to tell them she was praying for them too, but her prayers were so sporadic, and she was such a wicked sinner, she hardly thought God heard her anyway.

"You too. And if things don't work out with Andrew for Thanksgiving, remember you're welcome."

"I will." She grabbed her bag and walked out.

It was so nice to have such a short trip home, and less than ten minutes later, she was pulling in to her new place.

She needed to go grocery shopping though, if she were going to keep up her end of the bargain of cooking, and with the growing darkness, she wasn't sure she wanted to leave Dylan here by himself with Andrew and Uncle Ron. She wasn't sure she knew them well enough to be comfortable leaving her brother alone.

He was going to fight her though, because he hated grocery shopping. Steeling herself, she opened the door and walked in, weary after a long day of work but unable to relax like she wanted to. Not until the grocery shopping was done.

As she walked in, she was able to look straight down the hall into the kitchen at the far end of the house and see her brother sitting at the table with his schoolbooks open.

That was odd. Normally he didn't do his homework until she told him to. She walked down the hall, wondering what was going on. Something had to be.

A brown and black furball bounded down the hall and stopped just short of bowling her over. It brushed by her and went around her back, tail wagging and thumping, her face going up and down sniffing and trying to lick Reagan's hands, a constant motion that made Reagan laugh.

"Gladys," she said. "I'm so happy to see you too."

What a welcoming committee. Not exactly the kind of dog that would keep bad guys out, not if she welcomed everyone like this.

She knelt down, not that she needed to, and petted Gladys, scratching her ears and chest until Gladys settled and stood still under her ministrations.

"That's better. Relax. You're a good girl," Reagan said softly.

Gladys had so much excitement and exuberance it was hard not to smile at her, but it didn't hurt for her to calm down either.

After a few minutes of petting her, she straightened and walked down the hall. Gladys, now apparently her friend for life, followed closely at her heels.

"Hey, Dylan," she said as she walked into the kitchen, setting her bag and purse down and walking over to the table. "That's amazing that you're doing your schoolwork without me telling you to. Appreciate it."

Dylan glanced up, but his pencil never stopped moving. "Mr. Andrew said if I got my schoolwork done, he and I would go out and could start putting up Christmas decorations. I've never done that before. I thought it'd be cool. I'm almost finished."

"You can do that after you go with me to get the groceries." She couldn't make supper until she had the groceries anyway. And she couldn't leave Dylan here by himself.

"Aww, Reagan. He's going to start soon. He wanted to start before it got completely dark. Don't make me go get the groceries."

"I don't know him very well, and I don't want to go and leave you here. It's like imposing."

"It's not imposing. He wants me to help him."

Reagan wasn't entirely sure about that. Maybe Andrew had felt like he had to offer, or maybe Dylan had begged. Regardless, she couldn't just dump her kid off on somebody else even if he was her brother and not actually her child.

"Maybe when I know him a little better—"

"I'd offered. I truly don't mind and would enjoy the help."

She spun as Andrew entered the kitchen, a wary look in his face. Gladys immediately went over, her tail wagging and thumping as she did circles around Andrew's legs. His hand came down and absently scratched her ears.

"That's what I was trying to tell her," Dylan said, with more than a little belligerence in his voice.

Reagan almost said something to him about it, but she didn't want to have that fight in front of Andrew.

"I don't want to impose. But I do have to go get groceries."

"We just had sandwiches for supper. I'm sorry we didn't wait on you, but we were all hungry, and I wanted to get the Christmas decorations going outside."

Reagan had smelled something and now realized that's probably what it was. He'd been cooking eggs.

"I'm sorry you had to feed him. I can pay you for that." Hopefully he wouldn't charge her much.

"No. I offered. Eggs aren't expensive. It's not a big deal." He rubbed the back of his neck. "If you don't want to stay, that's fine. Or if you need him to help you and want him to go, that's fine too. I just want you to know that it's not imposing if you leave him here. I'm planning to put the kid to work, and that can pay for the meal I just made him."

He grinned at Dylan and gave him a wink.

Reagan chewed the inside of her cheek. She didn't have any reason not to believe him, but sometimes people didn't say what they meant, and she hadn't ever been any good at trying to figure that out. Did he mean it and not really mind, or would he prefer not to have Dylan with him?

"Fine. He can stay, as long as you're sure it's not a problem."

"It's not a problem."

She closed her mouth and jerked her head down. She wasn't going to worry about it. If he said it wasn't a problem and Dylan was fine staying, she wouldn't overthink it. She had too many other things to think about.

"Is there anything you'd like me to pick up while I'm out?"

"I have a list of groceries on my phone, and I haven't made it to the store this week. If you don't mind, I'll forward them to you. If you can grab them, I'll pay for them."

They exchanged phone numbers, and his grocery list popped up in a text. She transferred it to the notes where she had the rest of her groceries and tried not to look longingly at the chairs at the table.

Once she got the groceries, brought them home, and put them away, she could sit down and rest. Not before.

"Do you work full time?" Andrew's voice startled her, because she thought their conversation was over.

"Four ten-hour days. And I have one weekday every week off, but it changes, depending on scheduling, as well as the weekend. Of course."

"Just wondering. You look tired." He took a breath and then spoke again. "Maybe Dylan and I should go get the groceries. You take a rest. Uncle Ron's in the living room sleeping on the recliner. There's a second recliner in there, and it looks like you could use some time in it."

Right. He was basically calling her ugly. Probably she had black bags under her eyes and looked like an old, worn-out dishrag. Nice.

With Marlowe's words ringing in her ears, she almost laughed. She looked so exhausted he didn't think she could even go for groceries. She wasn't going to be the solution to any wife issues he had.

"No, it's okay. I'm used to being tired." There. That was the truth. Ever since she found out she was pregnant, that pretty much had been her life. Exhaustion. Her midwife had prescribed iron pills, but they hadn't made a difference.

"Send me your list. I'm doing the grocery shopping." Andrew didn't give her an option, which probably riled her more than anything.

"No." She wasn't used to being bossed around; she wasn't going to stand for it. She moved to her purse where she'd set it on the floor. "I'll leave Dylan here. But I'm doing the shopping."

"No. You're not doing any shopping. You're going to rest. It won't take long for me to shop, then Dylan and I will put the Christmas lights up when we get back."

Before Reagan could say anything, Dylan slammed his book shut and shot up. "I'm done!" He threw his pencil down on the table. "I can go shopping with you." His face fell a little bit as his eyes shifted to Reagan. "If that's okay?"

He was her brother, but he'd been so used to her taking the place of his mom that it was automatic for him to ask permission. She appreciated that. But he'd missed the point.

"I'm doing the shopping. And you can go with me if you want to."

"I said I was." Andrew's voice hadn't raised, but there was a new note in it, a note that maybe was meant to intimidate. But it didn't work on her.

Her eyes, however, did linger on him.

She supposed he looked like a firefighter, with burly arms and a thick chest. He didn't have the tapered waist or narrow hips of a younger man and was slightly thicker through the middle, which gave him substance. She liked that.

And how had she gotten distracted with looking at him, and admiring him, when she was supposed to be focusing on her argument?

"Send me the list. I'm going."

She shook her head, because his new, lower tone had somehow reminded her of their kiss, and the memory felt heavy and hot between them.

"I had today off. I didn't work all day, only to come home and go right back out. Plus, I'm not carrying a child with me everywhere I go. You stay here and relax. When we get home, you can put the groceries away, and you can make some kind of snack for Dylan and me for after we work on the Christmas lights for a while. Deal?" He lifted a brow. Those dark eyes swirled and seemed to see right through her to the tired exhaustion of her soul and the discouragement and fear that she kept carefully hidden from everyone.

"Deal," she said before she even realized it. She never backed down from a fight, and she never lost an argument. But she just had, and she hadn't even realized it until it was too late.

"The list." He nodded at her phone.

She lifted it up and started to do as he said when a new voice joined the conversation.

"There's that pretty little girl I've been hearing so much about. This your sister, huh, Dylan?" the voice said. "You didn't tell me she was cute as a button."

Cute. That wasn't exactly the word that she would use to describe herself.

"She's not cute. She's my sister," Dylan said, probably not meaning to insult her.

"Uncle Ron, this is Reagan. I think I finally met the person who's almost as stubborn as I am." There was a bit of humor in Andrew's voice as he introduced her. She held her hand out to Uncle Ron as Andrew continued, "Reagan, this is Uncle Ron."

She kind of remembered him saying that the reason he was renting the rooms was so that Uncle Ron would have company, and she could see that the elderly gentleman seemed to love people. The twinkle in his eye and the grin as he looked at Dylan was a good indication of that.

His gnarled hand clasped hers. "Good to meet you, girl. If you're almost as stubborn as Andrew, that means he doesn't have anything on you. But you look exhausted. How about you and I go into the living room and you sit down and prop up your feet a bit. A lady in your condition shouldn't be on her feet too long anyway."

Uncle Ron didn't wait for an answer. He turned, and she only debated for a second or two before she moved.

She didn't look at Andrew as she walked by him. She didn't want to see the satisfied smirk on his face.

"Hey," he called as she hit the doorway.

She stopped.

"Keep an eye on Gladys please. She gets anxious when I leave."

She turned and knelt down. "Gladys. Come on over. Come on."

Gladys wagged her tail, looking up at Andrew and whining. He made a motion with his hand, not even saying anything, and she gave him one last look before she trotted over to Reagan.

Reagan put both of her arms around the dog and pulled her close while Gladys licked her neck and ear. There was just something comforting about cuddling with an animal, and even though she worked with them all day, she didn't usually take the time to snuggle with any.

"She's taken to you for some reason. I noticed that yesterday. I'm not sure what that means, but I'm glad about it, because it makes it easier for me to leave. Normally I have to put her in a cage, because she destroys everything in sight if I don't."

"I'll keep an eye on her." She stood. "Come on, Gladys."

With a last look back at Andrew, Gladys followed Reagan into the living room.

Chapter Six

Andrew pulled into his drive, a smile in his face, as he and Dylan talked about the Cardinals and their chances at making it to the World Series next year. They had a slight disagreement in opinions about the new pitcher and also about the first baseman, but they were unified in their support of the shortstop and the catcher.

They were also unified in their hatred for the odious and cheating Cubs, and they'd spent a good and satisfying thirty minutes trash-talking the Chicago idiots, who wouldn't know a baseball bat if someone knocked them upside the head with one, and maybe someone should, just saying.

They were mostly kidding.

He hadn't enjoyed talking baseball with anyone for a long time. Growing up with sisters, he hadn't really had the opportunity. Not that girls couldn't be interested in baseball, but his sisters hadn't been.

It was something that he and his boys talked about when they came. He'd always wanted to do more with his boys, show them the mountain climbing that he loved, but he hadn't done that since Shane died, and Cheyenne had specifically asked him not to.

She was an attorney, and she'd gotten remarried to a high-powered attorney in Chicago. She'd make sure he never saw the kids again if they so much as broke a toenail doing something off the beaten path with him. He was very cognizant of that, and his kids meant more to him than the extreme sports he loved, so he quit.

Still, the baseball talk was fun, and they were talking stats as they went up the walk.

"Whose car was that?" Dylan said in a change of subject that Andrew had started to get used to. The kid's mind never stopped. He could relate.

Andrew looked over his shoulder. He'd noticed the car but hadn't really given it a thought because he'd been pretty engrossed in their conversation. He shifted the bags of groceries in his hand and wondered whether he should remind Dylan not to tell Reagan that they were standing on the back of the grocery carts and riding them through the parking lot.

Dylan wasn't stupid, and Andrew dismissed that thought.

If Reagan found out, it wouldn't be from him.

"That's Mrs. Hammond. She's our closest neighbor, and she probably came to meet you guys."

They walked up the steps.

"What's that music?" Dylan asked with one foot on the top step.

Andrew wasn't sure whether to laugh or be embarrassed. "That sounds like Uncle Ron playing his 1950s' rock 'n' roll. I sure hope he doesn't have your sister dancing."

Dylan rolled his eyes. "Reagan loves to dance. She used to hold her hairbrush to her mouth and dance around the house all the time." He shook his head. "She hasn't done it lately though. I hope she doesn't do it here. It's embarrassing. Especially when she does it in her underwear."

Andrew looked away so Dylan wouldn't see a smile. That was a side of Reagan he hadn't seen yet. Maybe he would. She seemed a lot more serious and careworn, and nothing like what Dylan was describing that sounded like a carefree teenager, dancing around blasting her music and singing.

"I'll keep that in mind. Uncle Ron doesn't exactly hold hairbrushes and dance around the house and, so far, never in his underwear, and hopefully Reagan won't convince him to lower his standards, but he does kind of get into all of those old dances... whatever they were all called."

He shifted the bags of groceries in his hand and opened the door. The music became louder, and it was definitely 1950s' rock 'n' roll.

He was almost afraid to look in. With Mrs. Hammond in the mix, who knew what in the world was going on.

He just hoped Reagan hadn't decided to move out in the last hour that he'd left her alone with these people.

He supposed he needn't have worried, since when he stepped in, he could see over to the left in the living room where Uncle Ron, with his hands reaching up and sitting primly on Reagan's shoulders, was dancing with her. They were doing what looked like maybe a foxtrot, but Andrew wasn't sure.

As soon as Uncle Ron saw him, his old face lit up, and he waved an arm motioning Andrew in.

"Come here, boy. Mrs. Hammond and I have been trying to teach this girl to dance, and she gets it, but she's too tall for us. You would fit her perfectly."

Andrew jiggled the bags of groceries. "Sorry. I need to take these to the kitchen."

"Aww, pshaw. I'll get those. You give this girl a partner she deserves." Mrs. Hammond stalked over and grabbed the bags out of his hands. She beamed at Dylan. "I brought pumpkin pie and whipped topping. Come on out to the kitchen, and I'll get you a piece. It was still warm."

That was all it took for Dylan to desert him.

He was going to have to have a talk with that boy about loyalty.

There he was, assuming the kid would stay. He had no idea what Reagan's plans were, whether she was going to live there for a couple of months or whether she thought this was her rest-of-her-life home. Maybe they should talk about it. He supposed most renters required leases. It just wasn't something that he'd thought about.

Reagan's eyes were steady on him as Uncle Ron dropped his hands from her shoulders. Maybe he was imagining it, but she seemed to be trying to figure out whether this was something he was being forced into and whether she should bow out gracefully. Maybe she was just thinking about how she didn't want to have to touch him, and maybe he should decline gracefully.

Or awkwardly.

Whatever it took to get out of this.

But honestly, he didn't want to.

He was curious about her, wondering about the father of her child, what was going on there, but beyond that, and beyond the kiss that he was never going to forget as hard as he tried, he could admit that there was definitely something about her that drew him. Something that made him want to shield her and would drive him to go grocery shopping, which he hated, in order to protect her from it and give her a break.

He didn't even know Uncle Ron had gone as he stopped a good foot from her and said softly but loud enough to be heard over the music, "You are supposed to be resting."

Her face twitched, maybe the beginning of a smile. "I was. But when Uncle Ron asked me to dance, I couldn't turn him down. Although I didn't know how to do the dancing he wanted to. Then when Mrs. Hammond came, they were able to show me. I'm not very good."

"Neither am I. I don't know why he thought I could show you anything."

He'd been around Uncle Ron enough to have a vague idea of some of the steps, but he'd never needed to use them. He'd just watched Uncle Ron with Mrs. Hammond over the years.

But the song that was on ended with a bang, and something

slower and softer came on. "I think I can handle this one. Maybe that'll satisfy him."

"I heard that, you whippersnapper, and you can dance the other dances. Don't you even tell her that you can't. Women want a man with culture. Dancing is a part of that."

"Do you mind?" he asked with a self-effacing grin. After all, it was his uncle that was pushing them into doing this. "I can tell him no." He'd stepped in front of her and turned his back on Uncle Ron, lowering his voice so the man couldn't hear.

"We might as well make him happy."

Did she seem breathless?

Maybe. He'd given her an out, though, and she hadn't taken it. Maybe she really didn't want to hurt Uncle Ron's feelings, or maybe she felt the same odd pull that he did, where he knew he shouldn't want to but had a hard time fighting the attraction or the strange desire to be closer.

"I noticed you didn't exactly answer the question." Maybe ten years ago or more, he would have had a little bit more confidence. But it had been a long time since he'd done any type of flirting with a woman.

Maybe his experience with Cheyenne had made him feel like it was pointless. The idea of falling in love then falling back out. If there was no permanence, if there was nothing a man could count on, if there was no loyalty involved, he just wasn't interested.

He was kind of fooling himself, because it probably was all wrapped up in the loss of Shane and the idea that he didn't want to care for someone like that again. Because he didn't want to go through that pain again.

And the guilt. Survivor's guilt. Why was he still alive when Shane was gone?

Those thoughts were almost enough to make him stop. But then, he figured it was harmless enough. She obviously had been with some guy she liked well enough, since she was pregnant.

Still, he wasn't exactly young and dashing, and he would be much more likely to term himself middle-aged and boring.

But he took another step closer and put a hand on her shoulder.

"Are you sure?" he asked, feeling like he still needed to give her an out. Not wanting to force her into dancing with him if she didn't want to.

She turned the tables on him. "Are you?"

She stepped closer and put a hand on his waist.

He'd never had six-pack abs, even when he was in top physical condition climbing mountains. He'd always been heavyset and a little girthy, and he'd grown more so in the years since he'd quit.

She didn't seem to notice.

"I am."

Funny that she was even asking him. He felt like he was the lucky one here, and yet she was kind of acting like she was.

He meant to put his other hand on her shoulder, but somehow it missed and kinda slid around under her hair, and his fingers touched the skin of her neck. He should have moved it, but he liked it there.

Her other hand came up and landed on the other side of his waist, and he wanted to suck his stomach in, which was a really strange reaction, except maybe not.

It was a pride thing. He resisted, and her hand skimmed over it, almost like she liked touching it, and slid around his back, and she moved closer.

He supposed this was where they could talk about all those things he wanted to know about her, but his brain and his mouth were not in time. Because he said, "I haven't told anyone about that kiss, but I can't seem to forget about it."

"Same." Her sugar-cookie eyes had darkened a little at his words.

"Every time I see you, I have to fight the urge to want to do it again."

"I fight too." Now she did look away. "But I know it's not a good idea."

"Where's the father of your baby?"

He could have phrased that in a slightly less rude way. Or not asked at all.

Her face tightened, and she stiffened under his hand. Instinctively, his fingers brushed the back of her neck, almost soothing. She didn't relax exactly, but she loosened little.

"He's not in the picture. Never will be."

"I see." He understood. At least he thought he did.

"Anyone around here?" He could say it was because he didn't want to have an angry father knocking his door down, but that wasn't it at all, and it would be a lie to even insinuate it.

"Trumbull."

"Is that who you were living with? And the reason you moved out?"

"No. No, not at all."

"I know I'm being nosy." He swallowed, and it felt loud. His head wanted to lower, and he wanted to pull her closer, and he was surprised he still had room to think as he fought all the things that he wanted to do but knew he shouldn't.

"Okay. I suppose it's not a secret. I'm ashamed though."

He didn't have any trouble believing that. She wouldn't look at him.

"Don't be." He didn't know the whole story, didn't know exactly what she was saying, but he felt driven to reassure her. "There were two of you there. And you're the one facing the consequences. Don't be."

She shook her head. "He was married. He told me he was separated, getting divorced. All lies. I was stupid. That's why I'm ashamed."

Her words seemed to echo in his empty chest, bouncing around and emphasizing the hollowness inside. Served him right. He'd asked. He was prying. He'd wanted to know.

He should let it go.

He hadn't wanted to. He was glad he hadn't. Mostly.

"Are you still in love with him?" He didn't even know why he was asking that. People fell in and out of love so easily it didn't even matter. In love one day, out of love the next. In and out, in and out.

Love didn't mean anything.

"I never was in love with him. I suppose I was flattered at his attention, and ironically, I thought he was well established and successful and would be a good person for me to be with and a smart decision for my brother and me. That bit me." The bitterness in her voice sounded foreign, and he doubted it was normal for her.

"I find it hard to believe that you didn't have some feelings for him but were just looking at him as basically a free meal ticket."

Her eyes closed, like something hurt. It bothered him. He didn't want this man he didn't know to still have the power to hurt her.

"You're right. I might not have fancied myself in love with him, but I definitely had stars in my eyes, which can make a person blind." She snorted. "Don't worry. They're gone now. I definitely see what he is and see how stupid I was. I guess I just hope I never do something that dumb again, but in the meantime, you're right, I've got the consequences to face."

He could see why she wouldn't want to repeat their kiss either. Could see why she seemed to be stiff-arming him.

"He must have been older," he said, wondering if it was someone he knew.

"Your age probably."

He pulled his head back and allowed her to see the humor in his eyes and tried not to be offended. "I think the lady just called me old."

Her lips tilted, and his heart flipped. "Mid-thirties?" she asked.

He nodded. Maybe on the upper side of mid-thirties, but he didn't want to split hairs over it.

"He might've been forty. I guess I never even asked."

"But you knew he was married?"

"Yes." She said it fatalistically.

"He told you he was separated."

"Yes." Her lips flattened. "And I stupidly believed him. I should have gone with my gut, but I wanted so badly to do something smart. To make a good decision. Obviously, I didn't."

The music ended, but he didn't stop swaying back and forth, and he didn't let go of her. He was heartened by the fact that she didn't either.

This couldn't go any further, he knew it, and yet he couldn't seem to stop wanting to ask her more, to learn more, to know everything there was to know, and he definitely didn't want to stop touching her. Through it all, like the shimmering icicles on a Christmas tree, glowing and twirling and catching the light, reflecting everything back and making it more brilliant and more emotionally intense, was the kiss.

He wanted another.

Maybe the way he remembered the one they'd had had given it more intensity than what it actually had. His memories could be faulty.

It hadn't been that long ago.

But she just confessed she'd made what she considered stupid mistakes. He didn't want to be another stupid mistake for her.

"I'm not looking for a relationship," he said, although he wasn't sure why.

"Me either."

"My wife said I was cold. Ex-wife. We're not separated, she divorced me and is married to a bigshot lawyer in Chicago. They're in the same firm." He had no idea why he was talking about his ex-wife. Other than maybe to let her know that if she made a mistake with him, at least it wouldn't be the same mistake.

She nodded. "I told him about the baby, and he told me to go to the clinic and have her taken care of. When I told him I couldn't do that, he told me he didn't want to have any responsibilities toward it, because it wasn't his choice to have it. He said to get rid of it. What he said made sense, but I don't have any plans to go to him for money anyway, because that wouldn't be right."

"It sure would be. Just because you didn't want to kill it doesn't mean that he's abdicating his responsibility because he told you that's what you should do."

"I could give her up for adoption." Her tongue came out and touched her lip, and she stared at his shoulder. "I didn't want to do that either. Maybe I should."

"I don't know. I don't get to see my boys much, because they live with their mother in Chicago, but they're the best things that ever happened to me. I can't imagine not having them."

She nodded, like she knew what he was saying was true. "I guess I kind of feel that way about Dylan. Sometimes he's a pain, and he's been a lot of work, but I wouldn't trade it for anything. I definitely wouldn't have wanted to give him away."

"You raised him since he was little?"

"Pretty much. My mom ran off shortly after Dylan was born. Our dad was in and out, and finally, after spending a few years in prison, more out than in. I don't even know where he is now."

"Some families are so screwed up. I'm not even sure why."

She huffed a breath. "I have a few ideas, but they're not popular." He ran his fingers over the back of her neck, and her eyes drifted a little shut. "That's so relaxing."

"Gladys likes it too."

Her eyes popped open, and they crinkled with humor. "I think the man just compared me to his dog."

"Maybe I'm just thinking about her because she's pressing against the back of my legs, and I don't want to fall into you. But I also don't want to let go of you either."

"He did. Just compare me to his dog. Well. That was romantic." She tilted her head, probably glad to be relieved of the intensity of their discussion. "Gladys is kind of beautiful in a shaggy kind of way. I suppose I could spin that into a compliment somehow."

"You don't have to spin it into a compliment. How about I just tell you I think your eyes are gorgeous, and when you look at me, I can get lost in them. And when you bite your lip like that, it makes me want to kiss you again."

The humor still danced in her eyes some, but they had darkened as well. He had almost convinced himself that it would be okay for him to try kissing her when Mrs. Hammond called from the doorway, "Are you guys gonna come in here and have some pie? I've got whipped topping for it."

He pulled his head back and stopped swaying, dropping the hand that was on her waist but reluctant to let go of her neck.

She did the same, dropping one hand but drawing her palm up and over his side and ribs. Not that she would feel any ribs, and he wanted to apologize for that, but he didn't want to bring attention to it, because she didn't seem to notice.

He thought, he could be wrong, but he thought she was the kind of woman who would love him the way he was, and he didn't have to try to be anything different if he was the one she wanted.

A new idea, and kind of novel, and he wasn't even really sure where it came from, other than his gut.

He refused to admit that he might have emotions seeping from his heart.

"Pie?"

She nodded.

Normally, he wouldn't have said anything else, but somehow his mouth started moving. "We're friends?"

"I think I pretty much dumped my entire life history on you just now. I sure hope we're friends."

He'd never kissed any of his friends the way he kissed her, but he was content with that for now.

Friends.

Chapter Seven

"Funny how things always get crazy right before the holidays, isn't it?" Doc Violet closed the back room's door behind her and shifted her purse over her shoulder.

Everyone else had left the clinic, and Reagan and the doc were the only ones left. There were a couple of emergency surgery cases that were going to need to be checked on, and Violet had made sure everyone in the back was good.

Reagan powered down her computer and put a hand on the ache in her back. "Is that the way it always is? I guess I block these days out of my memory."

They laughed together. It had been crazy busy, and they'd ended up staying over half an hour longer than they had been expecting.

"I don't know what it is about the holidays. Whether there's just more things for animals to get into, whether they catch the excitement of the people around them, but it's almost always busier around the holidays." Violet shrugged. "Good for business, I guess. And I ought to learn to expect it. But I always think we'll close up early and all have time to get everything ready for tomorrow, and it just never happens."

"Are you cooking a meal?" Reagan asked as she grabbed her own purse and pushed her chair in.

"My sisters and I. Our brothers are coming in, and our parents will be there." She laughed, her eyes bright. "It'll be kinda crazy, but in a fun way."

How nice it must be to have all that fun and family to look forward to. It's what Reagan had sworn she'd have in her own life someday.

Those prospects didn't look bright.

She'd just make her own family and fun. She could do it.

Violet stood in the doorway and waited for Reagan to walk over. "What about you? Do you have somewhere to go?"

"I'm renting from Andrew Coleman. You knew that."

Violet nodded. Reagan didn't expect her to remember every single thing she'd ever told her, but that was pretty common knowledge. Andrew was well known as the fire chief in Trumbull, well loved here in Cowboy Crossing, and well known because of being in the volunteer fire company.

"Our deal is he took some money off the rent, and I cook. He didn't say I had to make a big Thanksgiving meal, but his boys are coming in, and a lot of times, his wife doesn't let them because she wants them to have the big traditional meal, and so I'm going to make sure that they get it, so they can go home and give their mom all the details of how much fun they had at their dad's."

Violet's gaze shot up. Her head tilted. "Wow. That's considerate of you. If I were you, I think I'd be looking forward to sleeping all day tomorrow. But I love that you're trying to help Andrew look good. He deserves it. I don't know if I've ever met a nicer guy." Violet kinda trailed off and seemed like she was thinking about something.

Which made Reagan realize that Violet and Andrew were probably about the same age. Maybe Violet was a little younger. "So you and Andrew..."

Violet laughed. "No. I see him like a brother. He was older than us in school, hung out with our brothers and the Hudson boys, especially Zane, who's the oldest. So no, not me, but he deserves someone wonderful. I hope he gets it. Thanks for taking care of him."

Reagan shut the lights off as she walked out the door into the hall, and Violet flipped the hall switch as they walked to the front door.

"I've already locked everything up in the back. And everything should be locked down good and tight until Monday. Although, again, it wouldn't shock me to have a couple of emergency calls over the weekend. Like I said, the holidays seem to bring it out."

"If you need me, give me a call. I should be close to home. We don't have any plans to go anywhere or do anything."

They parted with holiday wishes, and Reagan drove home, thinking of the things that she needed to do. Andrew would have his boys, and she assumed he'd want to spend time with them.

She had almost warned Dylan not to bother Andrew while his boys were there, since he got to see them so seldom, and she didn't want Dylan getting jealous or trying to butt in. She hadn't though and was concerned about that as she pulled in.

Maybe she shouldn't have been. Somehow, she always seemed to worry about the wrong thing.

She opened the front door and stepped in.

A boy wearing a mask and waving an orange and yellow toy gun went flying by her, and she felt like she should duck. She did put a protective hand over her stomach and considered walking right back out the door as a second boy chased the first. She wasn't surprised when a third boy came ripping down the stairs and around the corner, barely missing her, as she put a second protective hand over her stomach and flattened herself against the door.

She just had to make it to the kitchen; she should be safe there. But then Andrew, a gun in each hand and a ball cap pulled low over his face, came running out of the kitchen and down the hall. Balls flew from each gun.

She blinked a couple times because he looked hilarious hunched over and running, guns crossed across his chest.

Okay. So she was smiling. Because it was just so funny.

He was a grown man. And was acting like a kid. He was so involved in the game he almost missed her standing against the door, and that was what made her laugh out loud—when he looked at her, kept running, then stopped so fast he skidded in his stocking feet on the hardwood floor, lost his balance, and landed on his butt with a plop.

"You're home early."

She laughed again. "I can see you weren't expecting me. I thought I told you I was going to be off at dinnertime?"

"I thought you did. But when you didn't show up at noon, I figured I must have heard wrong." He cleared his throat. "Um, so I was, you know, just keeping the boys entertained."

"You begged them to play with you, didn't you?" she said, her arms crossed over her chest, and tried for a stern look on her face.

"Maybe."

"He did!" a boy shouted as he raced through, balls flying, before his gun apparently ran out of ammo and he snatched three or four balls off the floor before disappearing up the stairs.

Reagan waited. There were two more, and there was no point in her moving until they were both through and followed the other one.

It didn't take long, and while Andrew did climb to his feet, he didn't shoot back at them, maybe because she was in the line of fire.

"I don't suppose your mother ever told you that you should do this kind of thing outside?" she asked, only half joking.

"I think my ex might have said that a time or two. I suppose that's why I really enjoy doing it inside." One side of his lips curved up in that lopsided smile that made her heart do something wobbly in her chest.

She had to snort again. He was gonna have her laughing if he didn't stop.

"I see. This is revenge." She nodded. "I'd better escape to the kitchen, or is there any place that's safe?"

Andrew opened his mouth, then closed it, opened it, and closed it once more.

"Maybe I'll just go outside." She turned around, thinking about the things she'd wanted to prepare for lunch tomorrow in the kitchen but deciding it might not be such a good idea if there were going to be balls flying around everywhere. Surely they would get tired of playing at some point.

"We can make the kitchen off limits."

She turned around and narrowed her eyes at him. "How about I make a batch of brownies? Would that sweeten the pie?"

"Make chocolate chip cookies, and I'll stand guard at the kitchen door myself." This time, his grin wasn't lopsided, it was full-on. "And if you make peanut butter cookies, with those chocolate things in the middle, I'll take the boys outside myself."

"What in the world makes you think I have any idea how to make cookies?"

He shrugged, a challenging look in his eye.

She pursed her lips. "With a deal like that, there's gotta be YouTube videos, and I'm not afraid." Her smile probably matched his.

But they waited too long, because she could hear the pounding down the upstairs hall and on the top steps as the boys started to come down, and the balls started flying.

Andrew heard them the same time she did. He closed the distance between them with four long strides and stood in front of her, wrapping his arms around her and hunching over top of her.

He smelled like spice and the outdoors and another thing that reminded her of goofy playfulness, which she wouldn't have associated with him at all until just now, but it went down good, and she breathed deep.

"I could've told them, and I will, not to shoot at women, but there was just something in me that couldn't resist the opportunity to be your protector. Even if they are just squishy balls."

She giggled, yes, giggled, and put her hands on his stomach, just below his chest, loving the feel of him. Solid and substantial.

He didn't feel rock hard or even slender like the father of her baby. There was enough of him that she hid behind him easily, and he somehow made her feel small, despite being eight months pregnant, and very protected, and she liked that feeling.

Her fingers moved a little, and he jerked, almost like he was going to suck his stomach in, but he relaxed, and she was glad.

Maybe someday she could tell him she liked him just the way he was, because she'd been around men who were more interested in what their abs looked like than whether they were having fun with their kids or protecting their women, and those men were boring.

Not that she was anybody's woman.

Why would her mind even go there?

Except it had, and the boys were gone, and he was still standing there, and she was still running her fingers slowly over his stomach and loving it.

He cleared his throat. "That was a little flatter back in my rock-climbing days," he said in her ear.

She wasn't sure she could joke about this, but she was going to give it a shot. She lifted her head up and raised a brow. "Mine was a little flatter just a few months ago."

His eyes crinkled, and that grin she loved appeared.

She returned it, then smirked. "I hate to rub it in, but I'm gonna lose mine."

His face tightened just a bit.

She swallowed.

If they were friends, she might be pushing the boundaries some, but she didn't like the fact that she said something that might have hurt him, even a little.

"I like this," she said, her hand stopping on his stomach, then sliding around. "It feels substantial to me. Like a good wind won't blow you away, and you're an anchor I can depend on." She moved her eyes away because she was a little embarrassed.

So she didn't really know what kind of effect her words had, if it was what she wanted or not. But she couldn't really expect him to understand. Skinny guys didn't hold any appeal to her, not physically. After what she'd been through, it never even really mattered what a guy looked like, not really.

"You don't have to say things just to try to make me feel better. I don't really have feelings." His words were brisk, and he stepped back.

"I guess you don't know me very well, because I don't say things just to make people feel better. If I don't mean it, it doesn't leave my mouth." Maybe her words were a little snippy, but how could they not be? He'd assumed she lied. It bothered her. She had a lot of faults and things she needed to change, but that wasn't one of them.

"Hey. Relax."

"I meant what I said."

"I just figured since you couldn't meet my eyes while you were saying it, they were just words." He looked away. "When I was rock climbing, I was in top physical condition, and so I know what that is. But since I quit, there's no point. Just good enough shape to do what I need to do for my job."

"I didn't meet your eyes, because I was embarrassed. Because it's not something I normally talk about with people."

He grunted. "It's not something I've ever talked about with anyone. Sorry."

"No. I am. I know I don't want someone judging me on my shape. People looked at me, before I was pregnant, and were angry sometimes because I was slender. Like I starved myself in order to be that way. It's just the way I was naturally. I didn't appreciate having people give me a hard time because I wasn't shaped like they were. Like it's almost a sin to be skinny or admire people who are or want to be that way."

"I get it. Seems like people enjoy tossing names around, without real substance to back it up. Sometimes you feel like you're in kindergarten with the new way people enjoy insulting others. It's unfortunate but true."

"It's definitely harder to overlook and give grace. I'm not that good at it myself. I suppose I shouldn't be complaining about others since I'm just as bad." She narrowed her eyes. "But, just so we're clear, while all shapes are fine, I like yours."

She tilted her head and looked up. She'd never had such an odd conversation with someone, but Andrew had been different from the beginning. As tough and manly as he seemed, it was even odder to her that they were almost, well, actually kinda really talking about his insecurity with his size.

"Don't hate me, but I do have a tendency to prefer the womanly shape without the basketball front."

She pressed her lips together to try to keep from laughing and shook her head. "I knew that. The basketball's coming out. Although, I have a feeling it's easier to take care of while it's there, even if I am exhausted."

His features relaxed even more, if that were possible, and she thought maybe he'd been a little concerned about hurting her feelings. "I thought we should have pizza for Thanksgiving. When the boys haven't been here, I've never done a big deal. But I did see the turkey in the refrigerator, and I assumed you were doing something. Let me help."

"How about I make some peanut butter cookies while you keep doing whatever it is that you're doing with the boys and guarding the kitchen door. Then we'll talk later?"

"Sounds good."

He backed up even more but then stopped. "Reagan?"

"Yeah?" she asked, looking up at him.

"The skinny girl with the basketball front is my second favorite shape."

"Thanks. Always nice to be told you're second best." He couldn't be serious, but her heart pinched anyway.

"The first best is whatever you are after she comes." That lopsided grin flashed before he lifted a brow and took the stairs two at a time, disappearing down the hall.

She shook her head and walked to the kitchen.

Chapter Eight

"If I get the turkey out, can you do the mashed potatoes?"

Maybe his words were a little terse, but Andrew was slightly nervous.

Uncle Ron had invited not just Mrs. Hammond but also two other folks that he met at the senior center where they went twice a week. Plus, his sister Athena was coming, although she hadn't shown up yet, and they had Preston and the three boys. His mind was so scuttled he couldn't even figure out how many people that was.

"Do we have enough plates set at the table?" he asked. "Maybe I should have pared more potatoes?"

"Andrew." Reagan grabbed his arm and tugged, moving him so she could reach his other arm, and when she had them both gripped in her hands, she shook him just a little. "It's okay. We'll roll with it."

Her eyes were serious, but she also had a slight amount of humor twinkling in them.

His breath huffed out, and he laughed, at himself mostly. "I'm just not used to this many people. I feel like something's going to go wrong and it's going to be a huge catastrophe."

"And we'll laugh at the memories in years to come." Her eyes clouded just a little, and maybe she was wondering where they'd be in the future. There was nothing permanent between them, not even a yearly lease. She could be gone next month.

He made a mental note to have a lawyer draw up a five-year lease and make her sign it. He didn't want her going anywhere.

"Right. We'll laugh maybe twenty years from now, but it will feel like a failure for now."

"You're not a failure. Sometimes things don't work out. But it's okay. Plus, everything is going to be fine. We've got plenty of food. You cut the turkey, I'll make mashed potatoes, and one of us will do gravy. The vegetables and rolls are ready, and we'll call everyone to the table. Easy peasy."

"Easy peasy? Really?"

"Sure. There's nothing hard about this. And it's not fun if you're stressing over it. I, personally, want to enjoy Thanksgiving. I'm having a hard time having a good time while you're having a meltdown over there."

He should be offended, but she blinked her eyes, and it almost seemed like she was flirting with him.

He made himself relax. "Wasn't having a meltdown. I was just making sure that we have everything together." His eyes swept the table, and his stomach clawed at his heart. "Did we decide whether we had enough places on the table or not?"

"And he's melting down again."

"Know that I'm mostly teasing you." He bopped her on the nose with his finger. She batted his hand away, and they laughed together.

He wouldn't have guessed, when he'd first met her, that she would laugh so easily. He liked it.

He also liked that she didn't stress about stuff. Normally he didn't either, but he could just hear his boys going home and telling their mother that they didn't have mashed potatoes, or somebody didn't have enough food to eat, or some other catastrophe happened, and she would call him an incompetent idiot as well as cold and heartless and emotionally distant, adding to the labels she'd given him when they got divorced.

"You're not cold and heartless," Reagan said over her shoulder.

"Was I talking out loud?"

"You were mumbling. I could hear you. I don't know who said that, but you don't have to believe everything they say. In fact, I would say, whoever said that, you can dismiss all their opinions. I'm betting it was your ex."

"You'd win." He adjusted the platter and stuck two forks in the turkey, lifting it out of the roasting pan and setting it down carefully. Golden brown with juices running out of it, it looked like it'd been cooked perfectly. Reagan had claimed to have done this a time or two. "I think I believe you now, when you said you'd done this before. This looks amazing."

She looked around behind his back into the doorway of the living room, where all of their guests were congregated watching a parade or football or something on TV.

His eyes followed hers. Two of the boys were wrestling. He wasn't sure whether one was Dylan or not, but he supposed he was grateful they were all getting along.

"We might have to taste that before the guests come out. We wouldn't want to serve them meat that was not perfectly done." Reagan's eyes went back to the turkey.

"You drooling?" He put a finger up at the corner of her lip.

"Really yummy food does that to pregnant women. Would you hurry up and cut that thing. Or do you need me to do it for you?"

"You are. You're drooling. My goodness. Better wipe that off. It's disgusting." He smirked at her. "Go mash the potatoes. Why are you standing here drooling over my turkey?"

"Give me a piece of meat, and I will leave you alone." It was probably big of her not to remind him that she gave him the best job— cutting the turkey. "Until I need another piece," she added.

Andrew cut a small sliver off, speared it with his knife, and held it out. "Happy?"

She pursed her lips. "For now." She put the turkey in her mouth and closed her eyes. "Oh yeah. I'm gonna want more."

"You can wait until we eat, just like everyone else. Five minutes tops."

"I can have half that bird eaten in five minutes. You better cut your estimate down by at least two and half minutes."

"Get the potatoes mashed, and I'll be ready to put it on the table."

"You're bossy. I like it."

"You're talking with your mouth full. I'd say I like that, but not really."

She laughed, and he loved that she knew he was joking. He didn't give a flip if she drooled everywhere nor if she talked with her mouth full. He sliced off a second piece and put it in his mouth.

"I saw that," she called over her shoulder.

"How could you see that? You're standing with your back to me."

"I'm a mom. I have eyes in the back of my head."

"You're not a mom yet. You've got, what, five, six more weeks?" He never had found out when her due date was.

"I've been raising Dylan since he was a baby. That counts."

She was right, but he didn't have to concede. He could just change the subject. "You don't have eyes in the back of your head. How in the world did you know that I just ate a piece of turkey?" he asked as he carefully sliced more and tried to focus on getting the meal ready rather than goofing off with Reagan, which was much more fun.

"I could see the reflection in the window." She shrugged. He looked at the window in front of her and could see her face reflecting back.

"Tricky. I'll keep that in mind." He took another piece of meat and turned away from the window before sticking it in his mouth.

"I'm looking right at you. I saw that."

"Will you swear yourself to secrecy if I share a piece with you?"

"I won't kill you in your sleep if you share a piece with me. Tonight anyway."

He handed her another piece and laughed a little to himself. He and Reagan weren't going to be eating any of the Thanksgiving meal they'd worked so hard to prepare. Neither one of them was going to be hungry after eating half the turkey.

"I'm on duty at the firehouse tonight, so I'm not worried about you killing me in my sleep. Tonight." He speared a piece of turkey and handed it out to her, sliced thin and dripping in juice.

"That looks really good," she said before grabbing it and putting it in her mouth. She turned the mixer on, and they didn't talk much more.

It seemed like him mentioning that he was on duty had seemed to take a little bit of the fun out of her eyes. Maybe it was his imagination.

Cheyenne hadn't been too thrilled about his twenty-four-hour shifts, either. That was a long time to spend away from the family. But the flipside was that he got to spend a lot of time with the family, because twenty-four hours on, twenty-four hours off.

"Hey, guys, I'm here." Athena walked in from the doorway, setting the pan of stuffing balls she carried on the counter before unwrapping the scarf from her neck and hanging it on a hook. Walking over, she bussed his cheek. He leaned over and kissed hers without taking his hands off the turkey.

"Glad you could make it, Nina. I don't think you've met Reagan. Reagan, this is my oldest sister, Athena."

Reagan turned the mixer off and held a hand out. "Good to meet you, Athena. Do I remember Andrew saying that you were the new nurse that was hired by the Hudsons?"

Athena nodded. "What a wonderful family. But yes. I think it's common knowledge, and I'm not breaching patient confidentiality, to say that Mr. Hudson's tumor was inoperable, and they gave him months to live." Athena's shoulders seemed to droop some. "The family hired me, and I get to spend the holidays at Cowboy Crossing. Mr. Hudson is doing well. That was said as a friend and not as a nurse."

Athena gave a friendly smile, but her words were serious. It was pretty obvious, to Andrew's ears at least, that she was the oldest. Always commanding. She was used to bossing everyone else around. Maybe if their family had been a little different, Athena would have been a doctor instead of a nurse. But as it was, she needed to get out of school and start earning money.

"Did you talk to the folks today?" she asked Andrew.

"I did. They're all good. Amber and Cecilia are spending Thanksgiving with them, so they're not alone. Sounded like everyone down there was having a good time." Andrew finished slicing the white meat and carefully arranged it on the tray. He grabbed a few pieces of dark to place alongside the white.

"Where's Uncle Ron?" Athena asked, looking around the kitchen and moving so she could see into the living room.

"He should be in there. Nicholas and Tyler are there too, plus a couple of people that Uncle Ron invited along with Mrs. Hammond, whom you've met before."

"Hmm." Looking back and seeming very, very casual, she said, "Preston? I thought you mentioned that he might be here?"

"He should be coming. If he's not too hung over. I don't think he's working too much, and when he doesn't work, he drinks." Andrew didn't mean that in a mean way, but it was the truth. Whether Preston showed up or whether he didn't was anyone's guess.

The thought was no sooner in his head when wind blew through, and then the door slammed closed. Footsteps echoed down the hall.

Reagan said, "Sounds like Preston's here. I'm ready to set the potatoes on the table."

An odd look crossed Athena's face. She and Preston used to get along fine. Preston had been several years younger than she and pretty much idolized her, which irritated her. She had babysat them both and treated him like a little brother, which was not the way Preston looked at her, but Preston wouldn't make any moves anyway since Athena was his best friend's sister, and he wouldn't want to rock the boat of their friendship.

"Hey, guys. Happy Thanksgiving," Preston said, his words slightly slurred, as he held up a bottle. "I brought this. My contribution to the dinner."

"That's a half-empty bottle of whiskey, Preston. Get it out of here. And you're drunk." Athena, her words snappy, flashed her eyes at Preston, her hands on her hips.

"Oh boy. She's in rare form today. Or I guess that's common form." Preston wobbled a little and waved the bottle as he spoke. "You don't need to get so uppity. I brought the wrong bottle in. I'll go out and bring the other one."

"You shouldn't have driven here to begin with." Athena took one menacing step toward Preston.

Andrew met Reagan's eyes over the table. He didn't want Athena and Preston to start slugging each other. His ex would just love hearing about that from his boys.

Athena kept talking. "Throw that in the garbage can, and see if you can't act half decent for the children. Better yet, you should probably go somewhere and sleep it off. Give me your keys first."

Athena opened her mouth to say more, and Preston smirked at her before uncapping the bottle and upending it, drinking it in a way whiskey wasn't meant to be drunk.

Before she could speak, Andrew said, "Athena. That's enough." His gaze cut to Reagan, and he turned his shoulder away from Preston, speaking softly to her. "Are you okay with this? I hate to turn him away. He doesn't have anywhere else to go."

"I think he should stay. Seeing someone act like an idiot shouldn't inspire the children to want to follow in his footsteps. We can talk to them about it later, but it might actually be good for them."

Athena's eyes narrowed at their whispered words, since she was close enough to hear, and her lips pressed together as her arms crossed over her chest and her whole being screamed irritation, but she didn't say anything.

"I'll be right back. I really do have a bottle that's appropriate for a family Thanksgiving in my truck." Preston popped the lid on the bottle he was holding and took another deep swallow before he slapped it back on and turned around, only walking into the wall once before he made it down the hall.

Once the door closed behind him, Andrew turned to his sister. "Nina, you know what happened. You can't blame him for this."

"I most certainly can. Just because something hard happens to you doesn't give you the excuse to hide behind a bottle and be too scared to live the rest of your life. Bad things happen, we deal with them, we get through them, and we go on."

"Maybe you do. Some people aren't that strong."

"It's a choice. It has nothing to do with strength."

"Maybe someone ought to reach out to him."

"You can't help people who don't want help. You can, however, keep them from ruining your life or Thanksgiving dinner." She tapped her foot and gritted her jaw. "I should have stayed at the Hudsons'. Preston is too disgusting to even watch. That kid had so much potential, and he could've been so much more than what he is, a sloppy alcoholic with no manners."

She took a deep breath and closed her eyes. When she opened them, she looked at Reagan. "I'm sorry, Reagan. I grew up with him, and he was such a good kid. Smart. And funny. Everyone loved him. He was athletic, everything was easy for him...just an all-American boy. It kills me to see him like this." She sighed. "I guess it brings out my mean streak. I want to grab him by the scruff of the neck and force him to have a brain."

Reagan shook her head sadly. "You can't help somebody who doesn't want it. But I think Andrew's right. We can be here for him. It's not going to hurt anybody. And it will help to show the children what they don't want to be. He'll help us to remember that we need to have empathy because I think maybe alcohol is the easy way out— at least it looks that way—and that's why it's so tempting."

Athena nodded. She was still obviously upset, but Andrew was pretty sure that Reagan's words had penetrated and made sense to her.

"You want to go call the kids, Nina? And Uncle Ron and his friends?" Andrew asked, putting his hands under the platter of turkey and carrying it to the table.

"Sure. I can do that. Just make sure that I'm sitting as far away from Preston as possible."

She strode into the room, every bit the confident woman that she was. Andrew appreciated her self-control. She could have made the dinner a misery.

He didn't want to turn Preston out. Sure, he didn't appreciate his friend showing up to Thanksgiving dinner drunk, but growing up, Shane had spent a lot of Thanksgivings with Preston's family. The three of them had been like brothers.

Time hadn't eased it at all for Preston, and maybe he hadn't let it, because he'd been hiding behind the bottle as Athena charged.

Still, she didn't know what it was like to have someone beside you alive and laughing and seconds later gone. Just that fast. To feel those last seconds, hear the screams, know there was nothing you could do, and know that your friend knew he was slamming into eternity, to have those seconds slow down and become ages, to know it could have been you, and to feel guilty because you were glad it wasn't.

Andrew had to shake those thoughts away, or he'd be the one ruining Thanksgiving.

The kids and adults came in, and chaos pretty much reigned, but it was a happy chaos, and other than the slightly dark cloud over Preston, who handled himself fairly well besides getting up twice during meal to use the restroom and not really eating anything, Andrew thought things went well.

Reagan ended up beside him as he sat at the head of the table, and he liked that. She laughed easily but wasn't silly, and her relaxed attitude helped him.

Halfway through the meal, he leaned over and whispered in her ear, "You were right. There was no need to get anxious. I'm sorry. Thanks for talking me down."

She leaned toward him and whispered back, "We had enough

places. And everything's delicious. Athena makes the best filling balls, and I'm so glad she brought them. Thanks for not fighting with her."

"That would have ruined the day, right?"

She grinned and didn't bother to answer his question. "It always amazes me how it takes so many hours to make all of this and only a few minutes to eat until you're so full you can't bear to eat another bite." She laughed a little.

"Have to agree with that. I guess this is really my first time making a full-fledged Thanksgiving meal, and I hadn't realized how much work went into it."

"And we're not done. We have to do something with the dishes and all these leftovers. I don't know why, but I always make so much, and then I'm wondering what in the world I'm going to do with everything."

"Better than running out of food."

"True. It wouldn't do to have your boys go home and tell their mother that."

"Right about that," he said with more feeling than he meant to. He used his fork to stir a piece of turkey in his gravy before he said, "How would you feel about going to the park for a little bit after we get this all cleaned up? We could throw a frisbee with the boys, and there's a trail to an overlook. We could take a walk."

Reagan's eyes widened, and her brows went up. "Are you telling me that's what you want to do afterwards with the boys?"

"And you. I'm asking if you would go too."

She laughed a little and looked back down at her plate, one hand going to her stomach. "I would look ridiculous chasing a frisbee around. Not to mention I've never been any good at it, even when I didn't look like I'd swallowed a watermelon."

"You could sit on a bench with Uncle Ron if his guests leave. You could still go on the trail walk with us. It's not that steep. I mean, if you don't want to, you don't have to. But I guess I was asking because I think the boys would enjoy it, but I'd like for you to go." His heart was beating hard, kinda like he was nervous about asking, which didn't really make any sense. It shouldn't matter to him whether she went or not, but he found he really wanted her to.

He wanted to spend some time with her. He also wanted to spend time with the boys before they flew out tomorrow.

They joined the conversation at the table as they ate dessert and the meal wrapped up.

The boys helped clear the table, but eventually Andrew and Reagan were left finishing the cleanup.

"Are you still okay with taking the boys to the airport?"

"Of course. The clinic doesn't open until Monday, so I have all day, and I don't mind at all."

"Thank you. I know any of the Hudson boys would do it, and Mrs. Hudson has helped me out as well, but I hate to ask with the way things are going with Mr. Hudson."

"You should probably visit him. As close as you were with his boys, I'm sure he'd appreciate it."

"You're right. Those are just really hard visits to make."

"I can go with you if you want me to."

It was his turn to be surprised. "Really? You'd do that?"

"Of course. Why not?"

"Because it's depressing to visit people who are dying."

"It's educational to visit people who are dying. We're all going to do it. I want to do it well. I'm guessing Mr. Hudson probably would be a good example of that."

"You can't be thinking about dying. You're young, bringing new life into the world. Dying is a long time away."

"We don't know that. And it's the last thing we all do in life. We want to do it well. I don't want to do anything in my life poorly. And that includes dying."

"You have the weirdest ideas."

"And we have the weirdest conversations. We talked about body shapes yesterday. I've never spoken about that with anyone in my life before. Yet you and I had a whole conversation about that. And now we're talking about dying," she said, shaking her head.

"On Thanksgiving, no less. And you're telling me that I need to do it well. I don't want to do it at all."

"This isn't an area where you get your 'want to.' You're going to do it. You might as well focus on doing it as well as you can and giving it your best shot."

"That sounds like suicide."

"No. No way. Never. I'm just saying, all your life, you want to do things so that people can look at you and follow you and do what you're doing, because you're doing it to the best of your ability. Living. But all of your living, all of your life, is focused on dying. Because that's how you're going to end. That's how everyone ends. You want it to be done well."

He'd never met anyone quite like her. He just stared at her, shaking his head slowly but thinking about what she said. It made sense. She was right. The last thing that he was ever going to do was die. "First impressions. Last impressions. They're both important."

"That's right. Everyone who sees you end is going to remember how you die. What are they going to remember?"

"This should be a depressing conversation." He was honestly surprised it wasn't. "But it's actually inspiring. I need to think about it. Because you're right. And I definitely want to go see Mr. Hudson."

"I'll go with you."

"And to the park this afternoon?"

"Yes. Once we're finished here, let's go to the park. But then I get to take a nap."

"When we get back, it's going to be time for bed. For you. Could be time for me to go to work."

She nodded, looking down at the dish towel in her hand.

Again, he thought about his twenty-four-hour shifts and how hard they had been on Cheyenne. He'd applied for that other job... maybe he should think seriously about a career change.

Chapter Nine

Reagan sat on the park bench, watching Andrew throw the frisbee with Nicholas and Tyler and Dylan.

She'd been a little concerned that Dylan would get left in the dust, because he hadn't played frisbee much in his life at all, that she knew of. But he seemed to be doing okay, and she'd been having a good time cheering them on.

Andrew tried to talk her into playing a little, and if she hadn't been pregnant, she would definitely have been out there even though she'd never played frisbee, either.

It was almost as fun to watch them and to watch Gladys as she ran back and forth, barking and yapping and jumping between them, having the time of her life, too.

The temperatures were decent, but maybe everyone else was taking a Thanksgiving Day nap, because the park wasn't busy.

Andrew had said that he and his boys had done a good bit of frisbee playing together when they were there. She got the feeling that he'd wanted to talk more about what he and his boys had done or maybe what he wanted to do with them, but he hadn't had time, and she didn't press. Maybe, there'd be more time to talk on other days.

She didn't want to take up any more time since he had a limited amount to spend with his kids.

Her back had started to ache, and she adjusted her position, running her hand over her stomach. Gladys seemed determined to get caught in Tyler's legs, and just as Reagan was thinking she should call her over, Tyler swerved, chasing the frisbee, and tripped over Gladys, sprawling out facedown on the ground.

Reagan gasped, and stood, but didn't run over, since he was old enough to probably not want her to make a big deal about it.

He lay there for a few seconds, which felt like forever, until he moved. Reagan let out a sigh of relief. Gladys sniffed all over him, nosing his head, almost as though she were apologizing, and Reagan felt almost as bad for the dog as she did for the boy.

Andrew had gone over and picked up the frisbee, but he didn't walk over to Tyler either, instead calling, "Hey, kid, you okay?"

Reagan almost grinned at the casual way men approached parenting.

It was probably the better way, because it was never good to baby kids, but she still wanted to check him out to make sure nothing was broken.

Tyler pushed up to his knees.

"I'm good." He shoved up a little more, until he was standing. "I'm gonna sit down for a minute. I'm fine, just need to catch my breath."

He walked carefully over to the bench, his hand on his stomach, and sat down beside Reagan.

He gave her what probably could pass for a smile, but it looked droopy and sore.

She scratched at her face. "That looked like a pretty hard fall."

"Yeah. Knocked the air right out of me."

The other boys had started throwing again, but she noticed Andrew kept looking over. She lifted a few fingers to let him know that she was on it, and he jerked his chin.

Tyler had no idea they just communicated about him as he put his elbows on his knees and bent over.

"It's just your breath?" Reagan asked as casually as she could. "No sharp pain anywhere?"

She didn't think he'd sprained an ankle or anything, but she thought it would be a good idea to make sure. If he needed to go to the ER, she wanted Andrew to get on it before he had to go to work.

"No. No pain. Just tripped over the dumb dog, although she wants to play so bad I can't help but feel bad for her."

"You're so right. I think she would probably be good at learning things, maybe even catching the frisbee, but it's gonna take a little bit of time to teach her. Maybe use a tennis ball to start out with."

"You think?" He looked at her, then over at Gladys.

Reagan nodded, trying to continue to be casual. She had three brothers, and in her experience, they kind of shut down when a girl got all excited. They also wanted to make their own decisions, so for her to tell Tyler what to do was probably pointless.

Her eyes drifted over, and she saw a plastic ice-cream container with a little bit of ice cream left in it, sitting halfway between the bench and the garbage can. She made a mental note that when she got up she'd pick it up and throw it in the can.

"You boys could probably work with her at the house, even tonight after your dad goes to work. And again tomorrow before we go to the airport. I think Gladys will be a quick study, because she's super intelligent. She just has those anxiety issues."

"Yeah. I noticed that. Dad mentioned it in some of our texts and even sent a few pictures of things she's destroyed. I've made sure to keep my stuff away from her, because she's not afraid to rip things up."

"That's true. I think part of it is she's anxious, but I think another part of it is she's bored. If you guys work with teaching her stuff, it might help."

Tyler nodded thoughtfully. "I'm not sure where to start?" He looked at Reagan like she might somehow know how to train a dog.

She held her hands up. "I work for a vet, yes. But I don't have any insight or knowledge on dog training. We never had dogs growing up." Her brain spun with ideas. "We could probably look at videos on YouTube. Maybe not now, but this evening after your dad leaves for work, we could try."

"Do you think there'll be enough time to work with her tonight?"

"Sure. We'll turn the floodlights on and work with her outside. I do think though, even though I don't really know much of anything about it, it's gonna take a while. A couple of sessions isn't going to be enough to turn her into a pro. This can take time and patience. When I say she's smart and will learn fast, I mean not like a day." Reagan lifted her hands and shrugged her shoulders. She didn't know exactly how long they could expect it to take.

Tyler had taken the idea and run with it. She could see the excitement in his eyes and the ideas that seemed to turn through his head. "I can't wait to get home and start figuring out what we can do. I think that'll be a lot of fun. And that'll give Gladys something to do, so she's not bored. And maybe it will make her forget about being anxious."

"I think that's a great idea."

Tyler gave her a big grin, a real one this time, before he said, "I feel a lot better. I'm going to go back out and play. Thanks."

He jumped up and ran off.

Reagan watched him go, a smile on her face. Andrew had some really sweet kids that were growing into good men. She wanted to make a point to tell him, especially because she knew it was hard for him to have them growing up without him.

It was probably a half an hour later when they quit throwing the frisbee and came over to the bench, everyone grabbing some of the water that she'd brought.

"How do you feel about taking the hike up to the overlook?" Andrew asked. "It's not long. Just a half an hour or so, and it's not too steep."

She wasn't sure what the look in his eye meant, but he'd already said he really wanted her to go. Which, she had to be honest, made her want to go more than the idea of seeing a beautiful view.

She met his eyes and smiled.

He grinned back. "I think she's gonna do it."

"You might end up carrying me," she warned, not really meaning it. Although the idea that she might not make it to the top kind of rolled around in her head. It wasn't wise to think that she might not make it before she even started, but she liked even less the idea of not trying.

"It's a deal. You boys got that?" He looked around at the boys that were chugging their waters. "I can't carry you guys, because I'll be carrying Reagan."

"I don't need you to carry me. If anything, it'll be me carrying you." Nicholas smirked at his dad, looking for all the world like a cocky teenager who thought he could conquer anything.

It reminded Reagan so much of her older brothers. She bit her lip to keep from smiling over it.

"Reagan. You can't make him carry you," Dylan said, with a hand on his hip and lip pulled back, looking at her just like a little brother should.

"He offered. Why can't I take him up on it?" she said, hefting herself off the bench and trying not to feel like a beached whale.

She still had four more weeks to go. And she, apparently, was taking a hike up the hill. Starting out feeling like a beached whale probably wasn't the best foot to start on. Or fin. Or whatever.

"Reagan said that maybe we could start teaching Gladys some tricks. Like how to catch a ball and maybe even teach her how to play frisbee. I want to go home so we can watch YouTube videos and figure out how to start training her." Tyler stood beside his dad with an eager look on his face.

"Well then, we won't take very long. We'll get this walk in and go home and see if we can find some good YouTube videos before I have to go to work."

"Yay!" Tyler said before he turned. "Gladys! Come here, girl!"

Reagan looked around for the plastic container she was going to throw into the garbage can. It had been right there. But she didn't see it anymore.

She searched the area, thinking that maybe one of the boys kicked it, but it wasn't anywhere around or even under the bench.

"Did you lose something?" Andrew asked, waiting for her while the boys ran on ahead toward where the arrow pointed for the trail to start.

"There was some garbage on the ground I was going to pick up, but I don't see it anymore. Sorry. Don't let me hold you up."

"You're not holding me up," he said, holding his hand out for her. His face was a little ruddy, and there was a slight sheen of perspiration on his forehead. His ball cap was pulled down, and his grin was boyish and endearing.

Reagan's heart twisted.

What they were doing today could be something that any actual family could do on a Thanksgiving afternoon.

She wondered, not for the first time, if her baby might not be better off if she gave her up. Surely there were other families who did things like this, with a mom and a dad and siblings who would love to welcome a new little one into their home, where she would grow up with a dad who loved to throw frisbees, and a mom who took walks with them, and brothers who played with their dog and taught it tricks.

Of course that's what they were doing today, but they weren't really a family, and they never would be. Not with Tyler and Nicholas not even living with them, and Dylan and her only renting rooms with Andrew. It could end any time. She wanted something stable and permanent for her child.

Shaking those thoughts off, she studied Andrew's outstretched hand and assumed he was holding it out for her. For her to slide hers into, and clasp his fingers, and have their joined hands between them like...like they were more than friends.

The thought made her eyes widen, and it scared her some too.

She didn't want to start thinking they were more than what they were.

She didn't want to start a relationship she wasn't ready for.

She had a baby coming. She didn't have time for relationships. She needed to focus. That was where she ran into these problems to begin with.

But the idea of having someone beside her, the idea of walking together, of...being a family, seemed to be represented in his outstretched hand, and she loved that. She wanted that.

Maybe she was being foolish. Maybe she was making another bad decision, but she went with her gut and lifted her hand, slipping it into his.

Their eyes met, and a current of awareness seemed to shift between them.

He didn't linger but tugged her hand and followed the boys to the trail, which was a gradual ascent, with several places of steep climbing but nothing long, and just exactly what he'd said—a fifteen-minute walk.

The overlook was stunning, and they stood for a while as the boys walked to the edge and took pictures with their phones.

"Have you come here much?" she asked. He seemed like he was pretty familiar with the area.

"I have. I guess I haven't been here for a while. When I was younger, growing up on the farm, I never really wanted to be a farmer. Always wanted to be an adventurer. I loved the danger and excitement. It's addicting. This wasn't exactly dangerous or exciting, but I guess it represented a common dream."

He seemed to be thoughtful, pensive even. Maybe it had to do with their conversation about death earlier. But she didn't ask. It seemed like a depressing subject to talk about on a holiday or any day. She wasn't going to bring it up again. She had some weird ideas. So she just stood beside him and tried to think of something casual she could talk about that wouldn't be depressing.

"So you went off and did what you had planned?" She thought he'd said he had left the farm for a while.

He nodded. "Some buddies and I worked when we had to and saved up money to do different crazy things—rock and mountain climbing mostly. Preston was one. I suppose he still does some extremely dangerous stuff. He leads whitewater rafting tours through the Ozarks down south, and in the winter, he still goes to Alaska. I think he's raced sled dogs up there." He grinned a little. "I have to admit the cold put me off. I'm not real big on freezing to death. Although any peaks over 8000 feet, you're going to get cold."

"So you've done high peaks?"

"A few." He lifted a shoulder and looked out across the view, contemplative. "We mostly did rock climbing. Straight, vertical walls. Untethered. Rope work." His jaw clenched a little when he looked down. "Haven't done it in a long time."

"Hey, Dad? Can we go home now? I want to get those YouTube videos for Gladys." Tyler came over and grabbed a hold of his dad's arm.

Andrew seemed to shake himself. Reagan regretted the interruption. There was something going on there, and she kinda suspected it had something to do with Preston too.

Andrew and Preston had been through something hard together and handled it differently. She wasn't sure exactly what and wanted to find out.

"Sure, son. Let's go home so I can grab some things and get you guys set up before I have to leave."

Chapter Ten

"They really wore her out," Andrew said as he grabbed the cooler Reagan had packed for him and got ready to walk out the door.

Gladys lay sprawled on the floor, panting.

He looked a little closer. Was that drool on her face? She didn't usually drool.

Just then she whined and scrunched up almost as though she were in pain.

"That's odd," he said, bending down beside her and putting his hand on her head. She barely lifted it. Usually she whined and was extremely anxious when he was about to step out. That changed a little since Reagan had moved in, but she still hated to see him leave.

"Do you think they wore her out so much that she doesn't even care that I'm leaving?" he said softly and then looked up at Reagan who stood beside him.

The boys, after playing with Gladys for several hours, had all gone down to the basement to play video games. They even dragged Uncle Ron along and were teaching him how to play. Andrew actually wished he could stay home from work just so he could watch that.

That wasn't the only reason he wanted to stay home from work, but seeing Uncle Ron play video games would have been very interesting. The old man was looking pretty spry after spending the morning with his friends and the afternoon sleeping soundly in front of the TV. He'd probably last as long as the boys did this evening.

Gladys whined again, and his mind went back to her.

Reagan had knelt down, awkwardly, he'd noticed. It was a little funny to watch her, but he was careful not to laugh, because he supposed that would hurt her feelings.

He certainly wouldn't want anyone laughing at him. He definitely had packed on a good fifty pounds more than what he'd weighed back when he was rock climbing and in peak physical condition. Maybe more. He didn't weigh himself much.

Definitely carrying that extra weight had changed his center of balance and made him less graceful and athletic.

The extra weight was unhealthy, and he should work on losing it, but he appreciated Reagan and her seemingly casual unconcern about it. Actually, she'd said she liked it, since it made him more substantial.

Would she mind if he lost it for health reasons? He almost laughed at that. Most of the time, he was worried about gaining weight and looking bad. With Reagan, it was the opposite.

She was definitely unlike anyone he'd ever met. Crazy ideas, crazy thoughts, crazy compliments. No one had ever complimented his stomach before. Not that he'd dated much since he'd gotten it.

"Andrew, I think there's something wrong with her." Reagan's body hadn't moved, other than her hand stroking Gladys's face, but the tone of her voice sent a shaft of fear through him.

"Really wrong?" he asked, although from her tone he already knew the answer.

She was scared.

"Yes. I'm not sure, but I definitely think we need to call Violet."

She was the one who worked at the vet clinic; she would know. He didn't hesitate to pull out his phone.

"You have her number?" He was already searching for it, but she rattled it off from memory.

"That's her personal cell phone." She paused for just a second, then she said, "Actually. Wait. Let me call from my phone. I know she'll answer."

He hadn't clicked the green button yet, and so he waited. Gladys whined again, and it felt like forever until Reagan said, "Hello. Violet?"

A pause.

"Yes, it's Reagan." She gave a little laugh that sounded more nervous than humorous. "I know you knew that someone was going to be calling you for an emergency. I'm sorry that it's me. But there's something wrong with our German Shepherd-Husky mix...she was just in for shots not that long ago. I'm not sure exactly what it is, but I think it might be a digestive problem."

Andrew wanted to pace while he waited, but he made himself be still, with his hand on Gladys. Maybe it was just his imagination, but she seemed a little calmer with him touching her.

"Thank you so much. We'll be right in." Reagan turned worried eyes on him. "She didn't even ask for symptoms. Just said to bring her in. I feel like time is of the essence."

"Let's go." Andrew spoke as he put his arms under Gladys, who didn't lift her head off the floor but whined when he lifted her. "Go get the door."

Reagan clumsily lifted herself off the floor, then hurried as quickly as she could to the door. As she was walking, she said, "What about work?"

"I'll call someone on the way and ask them to cover for me. This is an emergency. I have to at least get her into the clinic. There's no way you're carrying her."

Some of the worry lines between her eyes eased. She gave a

tremulous smile as he strode through the door with Gladys in his arms.

He tried for a reassuring look but knew he probably failed. "I think you're right. I'm not sure what's wrong, but it's scaring me."

"Me too. I'm so glad you're gonna be here."

She hurried off the porch beside him and walked ahead, opening the back passenger door of her car, and he eased Gladys onto the seat.

"You can drive," she said as she opened the passenger door and got in.

He hurried around, his heart feeling shaky and tender in his chest. He hadn't even had Gladys that long, and most of that time, she'd been bent on destroying everything he owned. But somehow, he'd fallen in love with the stupid thing, and he was scared to death that something was going to happen to her.

This was exactly why he didn't allow himself to get attached to anything. If the dog died, it was going to hurt painfully.

He opened the door and sat down, reaching for the ignition.

Reagan said, "I texted Dylan and told him to let Uncle Ron and Nicholas and Tyler know that we'll be at the vet's. I let them know what was going on."

Her phone buzzed as she was talking, and she looked down. She sighed. "They want to know what's wrong. I don't want to tell them anything that's not true, but I don't want them to worry or panic."

"Just tell them we'll let them know when we know. That should do." He was already backing out as fast as he dared to go and pulling out on the road.

He'd driven to his share of emergencies. "We should take my truck. I've got the flashing emergency lights. I suppose I could turn them on. That might be abusing my privileges a bit, but it is an emergency."

She returned his smile weakly. It was just a silly little attempt at humor, but he appreciated her going along with it.

It felt like forever until they pulled into the vet clinic. Violet waited at the front door, and when she saw them, she pulled it open and held it.

Gladys didn't even whine when he picked her up and carried her in.

Violet started throwing questions before he even made it through the door.

"How long has she been like this? What were you doing today? Did she get into anything? Reagan, what can you tell me?"

"She was chasing the frisbee," Reagan began and told Violet about their day. Everything, including Tyler tripping over Gladys and about Gladys being fine for hours after that. She talked about them working with her some to chase the ball, and when she finally finished, Andrew had followed Violet to the exam table and laid Gladys down on it.

"So you don't know of her ingesting anything? Could she have gotten into poison somewhere? Do you have rat poison lying around your house? Could she have eaten something hard or sharp?"

"No. Nothing that I—" Andrew began, his hands clenching because he wanted to be doing something to solve the problem, not standing around.

Reagan interrupted him. "At the park, there was a plastic container that had some vanilla ice cream in it, and I was going to pick it up and throw it in the garbage can when I got up, but when I looked for it again, it was gone. I do kind of remember seeing Gladys in that area, but it didn't occur to me until just now that she might have been eating the ice cream or possibly the container as well?"

"Oh." Violet bit her lip. "Plastic? It won't show up on an x-ray, but it could pierce the lining of the digestive system. That would do it."

Just then, the door opened, and Samantha, the vet tech on call, strode in. "Got it figured out?"

Violet still tapped her chin. "We might just need to go in, if that's the best thing we can go on. If it has punctured her intestine, we could lose her. We might lose her anyway." Violet turned worried eyes on them. "I'm just being honest." She took a breath, blew it out. "I need to ask, how much are we spending?"

They discussed it for a bit, and Violet brushed her hands together. "Okay, good. You two can sit in the waiting room, but I recommend you go on home. Samantha and I will take care of this, and we will call you with any updates or questions. Does that sound okay?"

They nodded. Reagan wrung her hands together, swallowing hard as they shifted Gladys onto a board and carried her into the back room.

Andrew put his arm around her.

She trembled.

His throat felt scratchy, and his heart hurt. He fought it, because he hated this. He hated this feeling of not being able to do anything and the idea of losing something that he loved. He'd been through it before, and he didn't want to go through it again. This was why he didn't get attached. This was why he remained unemotional.

He didn't give a flip if that's what his ex-wife accused him of, because it was true. When his emotions got involved, when he started exposing himself and allowing himself to be invested in other people and things, he ended up getting hurt.

Because they left. Things died, people didn't stay. There was pain.

He hated the pain and the way his whole body felt like it was stretched out and broken open and on fire.

He hated what it was doing to Reagan too, because she leaned into him, occasionally shaking, like she was biting back sobs, and she slipped an arm around him, squeezing.

"She was so happy today. I just keep picturing her as she was—running around chasing the ball with the boys. And every time she caught it, she took it to you." Reagan's whisper was soft and scratchy, and when she was done talking, she looked up at him, like she wanted him to acknowledge her words somehow.

But he didn't want to. He didn't want to remember any of that.

He just wanted to go to work and get called out and be busy his whole shift, too busy to think of Gladys or anything else.

Instead, Andrew ignored what she said. "I'll take you home. Then I'm going to work. You okay?" His tone was brisk, and he regretted it, because her eyes clouded, and her brows wrinkled like she didn't understand, and then her face dropped, and she stiffened beside him, drawing away—not much but enough that he missed her and hated the way that hurt him, too.

"Yes. That's fine."

He wanted to explain. To tell her that he couldn't handle the pain, because he couldn't control it. He didn't want to deal with it. He didn't want that to define his life and affect him. He couldn't work when his heart was breaking.

But he didn't tell her any of that, just allowed her to move away, and opened the door so she could walk out.

Chapter Eleven

Reagan was flipping eggs over easy Saturday morning when her phone buzzed.

Violet had called late Thursday night and told her that they had done surgery on Gladys and removed the plastic cup that had perforated her intestine. Once they were finished, they'd given her heavy doses of strong antibiotics and sewn her up.

They did the best they could.

Yesterday, she called again and said Gladys looked like she was going to pull through.

When Violet's number came up on her phone, she turned her back on Dylan and Uncle Ron and Andrew and answered softly, hoping for the best but fearing the worst.

"Hello?"

"She's up today. I'm not feeding her; she's just getting water, but I'll be in here for another twenty or thirty minutes. If you'd like to come in and see her, you can. You know that's not something we normally do, but you work here. There has to be some kind of perk to that, right?"

"Thank you so much. I'll be right in." She ended the call and turned around, relief making her weak. She put a hand on the oven handle to steady herself. "She said Gladys was up. We could go in if we want." Her eyes went to Dylan. "I think you probably have to stay here with Uncle Ron, but Andrew, if you'd like to go..."

He'd gotten weird after they dropped Gladys off, and they hadn't really talked since they'd done that. He'd been at work all day Friday and come home late last night. She hadn't worried too much about it, since they'd not seen each other much. But they'd not said anything more than "good morning" to each other so far today.

His eyes brightened, but like he deliberately shut down, they dimmed and his expression closed off, so she wasn't sure what he was going to say when he opened his mouth.

"I'll go. You're coming too?"

The way he said it, it sounded to her like he wanted her to, but he didn't say, so she just nodded. "If that's okay?"

He jerked his head.

She turned back around and scooped the eggs out of the skillet, turning it off and sliding it to the back burner which was cool.

"Here are your eggs, guys. We kind of need to hurry, because she's not going to be there very long."

She set the eggs on the table.

Andrew had already stood and started walking toward the door, grabbing his hat from the peg.

She snatched her purse and a light jacket and followed him out.

It was raining, but they didn't bother with an umbrella. He went to the passenger side of his pickup and opened the door for her. She mumbled a "thank you" as she climbed in.

It was probably for the best. Whatever had seemed to come over him, maybe it was just concern and worry for Gladys, had brought him to his senses.

She had decided that a romance was out of the question, and she needed to stick to that. Probably he was just being nice to her because of her condition and knowing that she and Dylan didn't have anyone else.

They didn't say anything on the drive in or when they hurried through the rain to the door, which he opened for her.

The clinic door was unlocked, and they walked in. Violet was just stepping around the corner and gave them a cheerful smile.

"She's looking good, and I know she's going to be happy to see you." Her eyes went to Andrew. "I think this will perk her up. She seems pretty devoted."

Andrew nodded. "I tried some of the things you suggested to help with her anxiety when I wasn't around. They've worked. I thought that she was not doing her destructive things anymore."

"I don't know if it was a destructive thing as much as she just liked the ice cream and ate the entire container. She seems like a dog that doesn't do things halfway." Violet smiled, then shrugged. "From what Reagan had said, you guys were playing, and you were right there. So I hardly think it was her anxiety coming out. Maybe just she was worked up and overeager."

They turned a corner in the hall and walked into the back, where Gladys lay in her cage, the first one on the left. At the sound of their voices, she lifted her head and sniffed. When she saw Andrew, she whined and struggled shakily to her feet.

"She's up and looking great. I think she can probably go home tomorrow. Normally, we would wait for regular clinic hours, but, again, perks of the job." Violet gave Reagan a grin, which Reagan returned. Although she was pretty sure the worry lines between her brows didn't disappear. They were only partially for Gladys. Andrew just seemed so closed off. Unemotional.

He had mentioned that before, that it was something his ex-wife had complained about, but she hadn't really seen it. Not until the situation with Gladys.

Maybe thinking about his ex-wife and Gladys and the unemotional connection made things click in her brain, but it made her realize the issue was most likely not her but was Andrew's way of protecting himself from pain.

He loved the dog, and they could've lost her.

Maybe it reminded him that he couldn't be so open and willing to trust.

Something for her to think about, not that she wanted to figure Andrew out. It was better for them to be more distant friends, although she'd enjoyed the companionship that she felt with him, especially on Thanksgiving. And kind of wanted it back.

Still, she had her own reasons for not wanting to form any serious attachments, especially with him, and figured she probably should be happy that she hadn't fallen any deeper than what she had.

She didn't want to think about how deep she might have fallen.

"I have a few things to do. You guys can stay there until I'm ready to go. Probably twenty minutes or so." Violet turned and grabbed the chart off the counter before walking away.

Reagan opened the cage door and scrunched down in front of the opening, leaving room for Andrew, who crouched down beside her, one knee on the floor and one knee behind her back, touching her.

Her focus was on Gladys, mostly, because his position felt intimate, and she had just been telling herself that that wasn't what she wanted. Funny that having him beside and behind her felt so good.

"Gladys," Andrew said, his hand out, his voice catching.

Reagan didn't look over, but it almost sounded like he was trying not to cry, which wouldn't surprise her at all since he was such a sensitive guy. She doubted he'd even admit that. But just the way he treated Gladys and his boys and her, it was so obvious.

"Hey, honey." His hand ran over her head, and she licked his wrist. "She looks a lot better than she did," he said, his voice still scratchy and rough.

Reagan slid her hand over the other side of Gladys's head as Gladys licked Andrew's wrist again, then hers.

"I think she wants to come home with us," he said, a wistful note in his voice.

Reagan bit her lip. "Violet would probably let us take her, but it might be better for her to stay here. If she's in the cage, she's going to be lonely and upset, but she can't do anything to tear open her stitches or upset her stomach. If we brought her home, we wouldn't be able to take our eyes off her. She probably isn't strong enough to stand another surgery."

Andrew blew out a breath. "I think that's what I'd like to do. I don't work again until Sunday night. I can watch her until then."

"I can ask."

There was no doubt he loved the dog, and Reagan's heart hurt for him, because he was struggling, not just with Gladys being hurt but with his own feelings that were so strong for her.

In the end, Violet allowed them to take her, under very strict instructions, which Andrew promised to carry out to the letter. She wobbled precariously out to the truck, and Andrew lifted her up carefully and put her in, climbing in the back with her after making sure that Reagan was willing to drive them home.

She was; although she wasn't used to driving a vehicle this large, she'd do it for Andrew. She realized she'd probably do a lot more. Because seeing him with his dog squeezed and pricked her heart in a way she didn't realize feelings could.

Maybe she'd been wrong. Maybe it was already too late for her. Maybe she'd gone and fallen in love with the man who was afraid to love anyone.

Chapter Twelve

A week later, Gladys was almost completely recovered. They'd fallen into a routine.

Dylan finished up his schoolwork as soon as he got home from school, Reagan put supper on the table, and Andrew made a point to help her on the days that he was home.

In the evening after the dishes were cleaned up, Uncle Ron and Dylan played games while Andrew and Reagan sometimes joined them but more often did some work at the table. Occasionally Reagan read a book. Andrew didn't allow Gladys to leave his side, and he made sure to spend at least thirty minutes brushing her and giving her some kind of attention.

Twice, he was called out to help with accident scenes, in addition to his regular shift, which provided some nice overtime, and thankfully the accidents were fender benders where the most pressing need was to call tow trucks and get the disabled vehicles off the road.

He'd been at his share of fatalities and gruesome accidents and considered it the worst part of his job.

Friday evening, he was sitting at the table, petting his dog, after spending the day directing traffic for a sideswipe accident. With just another foot, it could have been a head-on collision.

The teenage girl in the car hadn't even been severely injured, though she'd been taken from the scene in an ambulance, but it had brought back memories and made him think about death and the fragility of life, and how he took his life and health for granted, only this time, instead of feeling like he needed to protect himself from the pain of being attached, he thought about his life in the grand scheme of things and when it was over.

What was the meaning of his life?

Maybe it was his conversation on Thanksgiving with Reagan that had shifted his thinking, but he thought less about protecting himself from the pain and more about doing something that mattered.

Not something necessarily that lasted, because what was the point in having something that didn't matter last?

But something that mattered, now that was worth striving for, even if it was forgotten by everyone except the person to whom it mattered.

Or maybe, there was more. More to life, more he could do, more things where his life could make a difference.

Uncomfortable thoughts, since for the last decade, his focus had been to get through life with the least amount of pain as possible.

He wasn't sure that type of thinking was the correct thinking anymore.

Laughter erupted beside him as Uncle Ron triple-jumped one of his kings and won the checker game.

"I never saw that! I can't believe I missed that!" Dylan said, shaking his head and putting his elbow on the table, dropping his forehead into his hand.

"My eyesight might not be as good as yours, but with the years come wisdom, my son," Uncle Ron said with a little smirk, like he was kind of making fun of himself and admitting that maybe he had won more from luck than wisdom.

Andrew let them talk for just a bit more, then he said to Dylan,

"I'm not sure where your sister is, but I know it's time for you to take a shower and head to bed."

The smile faded off Dylan's face, but he dutifully stood while gathering up the checkers and the board and putting them in the box.

"Time for old men to go to bed too. All this wisdom needs its beauty sleep." Uncle Ron took the box and carried it to the hall cabinet where he put it away before he started slowly up the steps, Dylan climbing behind him, chattering about strategy and chess.

That would definitely be something to keep them occupied during the long winter nights, if they started learning chess together.

Hopefully Dylan would be here through the winter.

Andrew looked around. Reagan had disappeared after supper, which was strange since she usually sat with him.

He supposed he'd been a little cool to her since things had happened with Gladys, and he imagined that maybe she had begun to return the feeling.

It was for the best. He didn't want to get caught up in a romance and feelings that were impossible.

She knew it as well as he did. He was exactly what his ex had accused him of being, cold and distant, and Reagan deserved someone who could be an emotional support for her. Not him, since his ex had been very clear that was a definite area where he lacked.

"You need to go out, Gladys?" He stood. There was no real rush for him to get to bed; he had all day tomorrow off, going in for a twenty-four-hour shift tomorrow evening.

He didn't have anything planned and wondered if Reagan did.

This nagging desire to be with her, to do things with her, was something else he needed to fight. But he tried to excuse it as wanting to be her friend, even though he knew better.

They walked through the hall, with him grabbing his hat and his jacket and Gladys trotting along at his heels.

Maybe she was a little less excitable, but no less clingy than she had been before her operation and ordeal.

Her hair hadn't grown back, and Reagan had been taking her into work with her on the days that Andrew worked.

On the days when he had to go in in the middle of the day, he dropped her off at the clinic.

Violet had been perfectly okay with it, and Gladys was great with people, although she spent most of the time in the little receptionist office, lying at Reagan's feet.

He opened the door and stepped out into the dark night of the porch, almost immediately seeing Reagan on the swing, sitting sideways with her feet propped up beside her, leaning back against the chain.

The outline of her stomach was clear, and she rested a hand on it as though it was hurting her, or maybe she was feeling the baby move.

She startled when the hinge of the door creaked and looked toward him.

"I'm sorry. Didn't realize you're out here. We wondered where you were."

"I'm sorry. My ankles were swollen and my back hurt, and I thought sitting out here with my feet propped up enjoying the quiet would be a nice break. I should have told you where I was going."

She seemed to give a nod to the fact that they'd been spending evenings together, although it hadn't been something they discussed.

He also realized that she hardly ever complained about the physical discomfort of pregnancy. Cheyenne had a lot to say about it, and he had to admit at the time he wished she just quit complaining. It seemed like something a woman just needed to suck up and live with.

Cheyenne had been right. He hadn't been the most sympathetic person.

He'd been in plenty of uncomfortable situations while climbing—freezing cold, soaking wet, excruciating pain. Step after painful step, being so tired he could barely keep his eyes open, but knowing he couldn't fall asleep for hours.

He'd been through that all, aching muscles, sore back, complete exhaustion, and more.

He'd gotten tired of hearing Cheyenne's complaints. Because, through it all, everything he'd experienced, he hadn't bothered to complain, because no one was listening, no one would care, and no one could do anything about it.

Yeah. He'd been pretty hard on his first wife. Not that he told her she shouldn't complain, necessarily. He just hadn't been sympathetic.

Emotionally distant.

He thought, for the first time, that maybe Cheyenne had had a point, and he could've been better.

"If your back hurts, I could rub it." He'd rubbed Cheyenne's more than once, but it had always been because she complained about it and finally asked him to. He didn't recall ever offering.

In hindsight, he should have.

He wasn't that close to Reagan, but he could feel the shock shoot across the porch.

"I'm sorry. I didn't mean to make you uncomfortable or go beyond whatever rules we've established for whatever kind of relationship we have. I just was offering to be nice." And to maybe atone somewhat for his unkindness toward his first wife.

She'd gotten him back – if they were keeping score, which he didn't think they were – because she hadn't allowed him in the room for either one of his boys' births. It had killed him to miss them, but, again, in hindsight, Cheyenne had probably felt like he didn't care about her and didn't deserve to be there.

Maybe she had a point.

Too late now.

His words had seemed to relax Reagan some, not that he thought she was truly upset that he had offered. Maybe she was just more surprised.

"I don't mind, and I'd like it if you'd let me," he finally said into the darkness. Maybe he could be doing more for her. Maybe that was part of what he'd been thinking about today at the accident that could have been a tragedy but wasn't.

The shortness of life. The little things he could do and offer but never did.

Reagan wasn't the only one that he could help, but she was here.

"I'd like that," she finally said.

"Do you mind sitting on the steps? It could be kinda hard to do that on the swing." Not hard, maybe awkward.

She moved immediately, swinging her feet down and standing before walking over to the steps and sitting on the second one down.

He moved in behind her and sat with his legs on either side of her, two steps above her.

He barely got settled when she said, "I guess I kind of thought you were mad at me or that maybe you feel like there needs to be more distance between us. So you surprised me just now."

She spoke softly but confidently, like she was stating a fact and wasn't afraid to point it out.

"Cut to the heart of the matter," he said, only half joking. She wasn't beating around the bush and wasn't giving him any slack for blowing hot and cold on her.

Which was exactly what he'd been doing.

"I'm not very good at pretending nothing's wrong when I feel like something is. Maybe I should practice that."

"No. It's probably better to live honestly. Because you're right, I had thought that maybe it was a good idea to back off a little. I lost someone close to me, and when Gladys was going in for that operation, I realized I had gone ahead and done the same thing that I'd swore I'd never do again, and that was get attached to something that could die."

"Everyone, everything dies," she said softly.

"I know. We had that whole discussion about death, and you're right. And I guess maybe I've been thinking about that and the fact that my wife had told me repeatedly that I was emotionally unavailable, and maybe I was. On purpose."

"Do you want to tell me what happened?" she asked, and this time, she did sound hesitant, like she knew she might be asking a question that went a little too far.

He brushed his fingers over the top of her back and down the sides of her ribs. Funny that at times she seemed so big and ungainly, but each rib pushed out in stark relief, and he could feel her backbone easily.

"Are you eating enough?" *That* was a personal question.

But again, because of Cheyenne, he had enough experience to know that it was important for the growing baby for the mom to be eating well. He hadn't really been paying attention to Reagan and what she'd been eating during the time that she'd been living there. Maybe he should have been.

"I'm gaining weight at an acceptable rate according to the midwife. Maybe not on the high end of the scale, but acceptable. She said since this is my first baby, that's normal."

Maybe there was a little disappointment in her tone. Maybe it was because she thought he wasn't going to tell her about Shane. But he'd just been distracted because of the ridges under his fingers.

"Upper back or lower? Which is giving you the most trouble?" he asked.

"They both hurt." She grunted. "I'm not sure which one hurts worse. I guess the one I'm thinking about."

He left it at that. It was probably true.

He rubbed between her shoulder blades for a little bit. That was where his back often hurt after a hard day of work, although his lower back was what bothered him if he'd been lifting things. He'd get to that in a bit.

Chapter Thirteen

The silence settled, and they let it as Gladys lay her head on Andrew's lap, sighing deeply, and the darkness wrapped around the three of them, with a few bold crickets chirping and the wind blowing the bare tree branches together.

Finally he started, "Shane was the life of the party and the glue that kept Preston and me together. I was a lot more serious and driven, and Preston was more likely to be a slacker, and Shane made us both laugh. He made things fun. He was a great friend, considerate, and always pulled more than his weight. Just one of those people that are larger than life, and I guess I never even really thought about it but one of those people that you're just honored to be friends with."

She seemed to nod a little, like she knew what he was talking about.

Maybe she did.

Shane wasn't exactly unique in his ability to make people laugh and feel comfortable.

"He made sure we had fun, but he also wasn't scared. Not to do the dangerous things, but I was the one who pushed the rock climbing. I loved that rush. Because there's nothing to catch you if you fall, so the success is that much sweeter." He paused, because his throat had closed, and his nose started to burn. "But failure is final." That was something that hadn't really sunk in until it was too late. Too late for Shane.

"I guess that was the lesson I learned with Shane that day. Up until that point, it had been almost a game. I knew there was danger. We all knew there was danger. That was the source of the rush. But I didn't realize how final the danger was until he was beside us one second and dead the next."

His hand moved down her back, and subconsciously he admired the curve, the graceful slope, the delicate strength.

There was definitely nothing delicate or graceful or slender about him. Maybe the contradictions drew him too. As he was sure they were designed to do.

The contrast and the differences. He wasn't interested in someone who was the same as he was; he loved the differences.

She waited silently, and he pulled his mind back to where it didn't want to go.

"I guess I was unprepared. I know I was. I'd never known pain like that before. And loss, and heartache, and the longing to just go back and do those last five minutes, ten minutes, week, year, whatever...everything over again, so the outcome would be different. I know I withdrew from my wife. We had two little boys at the time, and she'd been pressuring me to stop anyway. She didn't want the kids to get involved in stuff that was dangerous. She didn't understand my need to be in those things anyway. I don't understand that need. That drive, that rush I craved. I felt like she didn't understand me, and I'm sure she felt the same way about me in hindsight."

He could see Reagan's head going up and down, like she was agreeing. He wasn't sure whether she was agreeing that his wife didn't understand him, or he didn't understand his wife, maybe both.

"But that taught me, Shane's death. It taught me that I couldn't hold on too tightly. I couldn't love so deeply. I couldn't get so emotionally invested in other people, because it just led to pain. I vowed I would never feel hurt like that again. And the only thing I knew to do was to shut myself off. Which of course, Cheyenne didn't understand. I suppose that's what eventually led to our divorce. Neither of us cheated, although she is remarried and happily, I think."

He moved his fingers to either side of her backbone, down to her lower back, where he pressed carefully in small circles. If his back hurt, that always seemed to make it feel better.

He was pretty much done, done with the psychoanalysis, done with probing into his brain and trying to figure out why he was as messed up as he was.

Shane's death had a lot to do with it, but it was probably also his male tendencies to not want to get entangled with the messy emotional stuff anyway.

He thought maybe Reagan wasn't going to say anything. He also thought that probably if anything, she would side with Cheyenne, since women tended to stick together.

He wasn't expecting her words when she finally did speak. "Did it ever occur to you that maybe you learned the wrong lesson? Maybe God allowed you to see Shane die, not so you could protect yourself from any more pain, but so that you could know to live harder, give more, be braver, because life is short and opportunities to love and laugh and live are soon gone?"

How could she articulate so clearly the things that had been in his head the last week or so? That was almost exactly what he'd been struggling with, in a more nebulous type of way, because the words hadn't been there exactly. Not as clearly as she just laid them out.

"Isn't that kind of what you're doing?" she asked gently. "I mean, the risk that you took being on the rocks, the danger and excitement, was a physical danger and excitement. But isn't it almost the same as risking your emotions? Of living without fear? Of loving without fear? Doesn't it take bravery to open your heart and give everything you have to someone? Isn't that risky? Isn't that a risk that's almost as dangerous as clinging to a sheer rock wall, with no safety rope attached? How can you do one and shy away from the other?"

She hadn't turned around, hadn't moved, hadn't even turned her head, and yet the point she made was so profound he couldn't believe he hadn't seen it before.

Why was he brave in one area and a coward in the other?

"Physical danger is easier," he said for lack of anything else to say. But even he could see the hole in that argument, if he could even call it an argument.

"Isn't that the point? You want to do the hard thing? You want to do the dangerous thing? You want to stretch yourself and push yourself and make yourself be braver and do more? And yet you choose the easier thing when it comes to matters of the heart and emotions? Right?"

He didn't want to think about it. She was so right. But he wasn't ready to admit that she was. Maybe to himself, but not to her.

She didn't have anything invested in him, and he wasn't even sure what her point was, what change she wanted to see in him.

Or maybe she didn't care whether he changed or not, she was just making an argument.

"I don't know where you get off thinking you're so smart. Especially since right now you're carrying the baby of a man who doesn't want to have anything to do with you. You don't even have a house to bring her home to. You're just renting a room."

Her relaxation disappeared like smoke on the wind, and her whole body stiffened.

He wanted to slap himself. His words were so unkind and harsh. But she'd hit him, hit him with such a reasonable argument he couldn't argue back, so he had to do a personal attack, except he didn't have to. He couldn't seem to stop himself though.

So he did the next best thing. "I'm sorry. That was uncalled for."

"No. You're right. You're absolutely right." She straightened and moved away from him, standing on the steps. "I'm about the stupidest person in the world. I don't even know why I thought I could tell you anything. I certainly have no right to give you advice, criticize the way you've lived your life. I wouldn't take advice from me, and I don't expect you to either." She took two more steps down to the bottom, holding onto the rail and looking out across the night-shrouded fields.

"Please. I'm sorry. Your point was too good, too right, too close to home. That's why I felt like I had to lash out. My words were wrong. I'm sorry."

He didn't know what else to say. He couldn't take them back, as much as he wanted to. As much as he felt like they were completely inaccurate. Because it wasn't her fault, not any more than it was the man who'd lied to her. Maybe being gullible was a character flaw. Lying definitely was.

She hadn't taken the easy way out or what seemed like the easier way. She was doing the harder thing, and that was admirable and not something he should reduce into a crude comment.

"I'm going to take a walk," she said before stepping off the porch and walking into the darkness.

His phone buzzed in his pocket as he stood to follow her. Gladys whined, already on her feet and looking between Reagan and Andrew, as though she were torn as to which one she wanted to be with.

Andrew wasn't torn, he definitely wanted to follow her, although not only did he think he wasn't welcome, but when he pulled his phone out, he saw that the call was from his ex.

He took a fortifying breath before swiping and answering. "Hello?"

He gritted his jaw and leaned against the pillar, wondering where Reagan was going and running over the dangers in his head, trying to keep from following her down the drive to be sure she was safe.

There wasn't anything that was going to hurt her out there. But that didn't stop him from wanting to protect her anyway.

"Andrew, I'm glad I caught you. I've been meaning to call you for several days now. How are you doing?"

His ex was always civil, with her cultured voice and perfect manners. They'd never fought, other than her calling him names and making accusations, and even then, she always spoke in a perfectly rational tone, offering an almost clinical diagnosis instead of the heartfelt accusations of a wife who'd been neglected.

"I'm fine. 'Sup?"

He didn't want to have a long conversation with her. Maybe he'd been in love with her at one point, more likely just acted on his attraction, but she was married to someone else, and any bridge between them had been burned. He wasn't going back, wasn't interested in rekindling anything they'd had.

Common courtesy and civility were all he wanted now.

Plus, his mind was on Reagan.

She gave a delicate sniff, almost as though it didn't surprise her that all he could manage to say were three words.

"I just wanted to call and thank you for the Thanksgiving that you gave the boys. They said that they had a good time, and everything they described to me sounded like a nice traditional meal and holiday, which is what I wanted them to have. I've always been unafraid to criticize, so I wanted to be just as unafraid to compliment."

So, yeah, her words had made his brow shoot up in shocked surprise. Because, sure, she had always been unafraid to criticize and tell him how he wasn't being a good dad. Even though he'd been trying as hard as he could to be the dad that she wanted, since she seemed to want what was best.

"They did tell me that they had walked to an overlook, but it sounded like something that normal people did, and not one of your extreme things. I wanted to make sure you knew I appreciated it."

"Thank you, I guess." He wasn't sure what else to say. He'd never asked Nicholas and Tyler to lie for him, and he'd never asked them not to talk about him, but he kind of assumed that they probably didn't much. Once they got back to Chicago and their busy life there, he figured they probably forgot about him for the most part.

"I also wanted to say that Sheldon and I are planning a European vacation over Christmas, and I want to take the boys with me. I know that means you wouldn't see them, because we'll be gone for three weeks, but you can have extra time in January or whenever you want it. Is that okay?"

She always got the boys on Christmas Day, but he usually had them sometime in the week afterwards and often on New Year's.

She had insisted that it was important for them to be with the family on Christmas morning as they opened gifts. He hadn't had the heart to argue, just because he thought that the boys probably preferred to be with their mom on Christmas anyway.

He couldn't make it special like she could. He didn't think of all those little details, and the lights he threw up in the yard were the only decorations he usually did.

That thought made him think about the inside of his house and things he'd subconsciously noticed but hadn't actually physically realized. There were a couple of new pictures up in the hall. A little bit of garland, and a couple of plants on the kitchen window. Hot pads were arranged artistically on hooks over beside the stove, and there were just several other little homey things that had happened that he hadn't even thought about until he thought about Cheyenne and the details that she took care of that made the holidays, if not special, at least better.

Reagan did that too. She had done that with his house.

And he hadn't noticed, hadn't said anything.

"That's fine." He probably would never see his boys on Christmas. And that was probably for the best. "We'll figure something out. Maybe they can spend some extra time with me over summer vacation."

"That will work. Thank you. I will make sure they call you before we leave, and I will make sure there's a phone call on Christmas Day as well."

"Okay." He couldn't expect anything more.

They didn't have anything else to say to each other and made the usual pleasant noises before hanging up.

By that time, he had no idea where Reagan had gone, so he walked off the porch to the tree in the yard and leaned against it, waiting until she walked back past him into the house before he went in and went to bed.

Chapter Fourteen

By the time the next weekend came, Andrew had barely slept at all.

Probably in life there were times where things were definitely not pleasant, when a person saw themselves and didn't like what they were looking at.

Maybe those were times of learning.

He could see them clearly in his progression as a mountain climber and then as a rock climber, where he'd seen his technique needed work, or his mental attitude needed improvement, or even his gear needed to be updated. It was never fun to face what could be perceived as a lack.

Even less so when it was a personal lack.

But once one had been exposed to an area that needed improvement, it was irresponsible to ignore and go on with his life as though nothing had changed.

He decided that Cheyenne had been wrong. He wasn't emotionally distant, or stunted, or uncaring.

He felt emotions. Deeply. Maybe he wasn't the best at expressing them, but he felt them.

The problem was that he got so focused on his own emotions that he didn't see anyone else. Not their needs, not their feelings, and most definitely not what he could do for them.

It wasn't exactly what Reagan had said the night he rubbed her back. She had challenged him to be brave, to dare to do more, to not be afraid. And that was basically the stepping-off point, for him to see that she was right.

He'd been so inwardly focused, so scared that he might get hurt again, so selfishly protective, that he didn't stop to think that he was wasting the opportunity to share with someone else and potentially help them both.

Loving Gladys wasn't a matter of him risking his feelings as much as it was a matter of him reaching out to another living creature that needed him and giving, without thinking of the consequences, everything he could. Everything he had. Being brave, unafraid to love, and to show that love without reservation.

Because loving her wasn't enough. Love was useless until it was given away.

He wasn't thinking of love as a feeling but as an action. Because love was a verb. A verb he did on his dog, a verb he could do to other people, Uncle Ron, Nicholas, Tyler, Dylan...Reagan.

Maybe the gloomy weather contributed to his mood, since it had rained every day since he and Reagan had spoken, but he was definitely pensive when he turned into the drive of the former pastor of the white church in Cowboy Crossing, Pastor Gus Wyatt, who had recently lost his wife to cancer.

He'd sat under Gus's preaching for years when he was home from his excursions, but he hadn't spoken with him much at all since Miss Lynette's funeral.

But Gus was making furniture, and Andrew wasn't really sure how to make love into an action verb without making it concrete as well.

So he was ordering a cradle for Reagan.

Gus's fifteen-passenger van was parked at the house, but if he were Gus, he'd be at the barn, so Andrew didn't even bother pulling into the house but drove straight to the barn and got out. Not bothering to dodge the raindrops, he ran through them to what was the old milk house door and burst through it.

His hunch was right, as Gus was sitting at a table bench, sanding an already glowing rocking chair.

Gus's shaggy head jerked up when Andrew entered, the bushy beard and shoulder-length hair a definite difference from the well-groomed, clean-shaven, shorthaired man he'd been when he'd been behind the pulpit.

Several kids ran around, in various states of undress, and one who looked to be almost four wore nothing but a diaper, which looked to have been changed possibly once in the last week. Not that Andrew was any judge.

He wouldn't consider the children neglected, but they were definitely skirting on the edges of what society would deem acceptable.

The church ladies had tried to help, but Gus had kindly, but firmly, told them "no thank you."

No doubt it was just Gus mourning his wife and trying to become used to his new reality.

It gave Andrew pause for a moment.

That was what he could be risking. That was exactly what he was afraid of. Whether he admitted the fear or not. He could end up like this, completely devastated when the person that he loved without reserve left. Whether through death, or whether she walked out with insults and putdowns.

It'd been hard enough when Cheyenne left, and he certainly hadn't been loving her without reserve.

Gus jerked his head. "Hey, man."

Andrew nodded back. "Gus."

"Come on in, clear off a spot, and sit down." Gus's hands, which had stilled when Andrew walked in, began moving again, and Gus looked back down at his work.

"Beautiful rocking chair."

"Thanks." Gus didn't stop working. "Lynette spent hours with our babies rocking in the evening. She liked hers a little lower to the ground because her legs were short. This is the style that she most loved." Gus's words were soft, like the memories were sweet and sacred.

"Is it for sale?" Andrew asked.

"I think so."

"I'll take it." Andrew never bought stuff without asking for the price, but he didn't even consider counting the cost, not only because he knew Gus would be fair, but because something about Gus's words made him feel like Reagan deserved a man who would see her rocking their babies and want her to have a chair she was comfortable in. "And I wanted to order a cradle. I know it's last minute, but I wanted it before Christmas."

Gus nodded. "Quality furniture can't be rushed."

"I know. If it's not possible, that's fine."

"I can do it." Gus kept rubbing his sandpaper back and forth with the grain of the wood. "What type of wood would you like?"

"Whatever would match that."

Gus finally seemed to realize what was going on, and his head lifted, his eyes, shrouded with sadness, still shrewd and deeply caring. "Have I missed a wedding?"

"No."

Bushy brows knotted, and if it was possible to feel love pouring out of someone, Andrew could feel it from Gus. It was part of what had made him an amazing pastor. Not the beautiful words that poured out of his sermons, but the love that he had for each and every one of his parishioners. One couldn't help but feel it.

Lynette had been the one to organize everything and to make things happen behind the scenes. Gus had been the one to love everyone.

"Are you ever going to get over her?" Andrew asked, when he'd really meant to explain what was going on with Reagan, and that the baby wasn't his, and that there was no wedding because there wasn't a relationship. But somehow, that wasn't what came out. Probably because that wasn't what he'd been thinking all week.

"No. You don't get over a love like that."

"So that's it for you? There's nothing more?" Andrew didn't even really know what he was asking.

"There's no end. In the human capacities, love is not finite. God gives us more of what we give away."

"With the pain. How can you stand the pain?"

Gus looked down at his hands, which had stilled, and he seemed to be deep in thought. Andrew thought he was going to get some Bible verses quoted at him, but Gus finally lifted his head.

"You're right. If you don't love, there's no pain and death. But then what's the point of life?"

"But you've done it once. Surely you're not doing it again?"

"I suppose, if my life were about me, that's exactly how I would think. But it's not. It's not about me. And it's a waste if it is."

Andrew shook his head. "Then what's this?" He indicated the room, but he really meant the sad condition of the children in the unchanged diaper and uncut hair and the unkempt appearances.

Gus nodded like he understood, his eyes even more shrouded and sad. "God gives us time to mourn. But also whatever He gives us, He wants us to give away." He swallowed. "He can't give us more if we don't give away what He's given. Not just material things. It's love and compassion and caring and concern. And it hurts, if we do it right, but all those painful experiences draw us closer to the Lord."

As a Christian, being closer to the Lord was supposed to be the goal, he knew it, but Andrew wasn't sure the pain was worth it.

Gus shook his head. "We pay for love with pain. If we close ourselves off to love because we're afraid of the pain, we close ourselves off to what makes life truly worth living. And then what's left? There's nothing worth protecting, nothing worth living for, nothing of any worth left if we close ourselves off from loving. It's ironic, sure, but it's true as I sit here."

The kid who'd been wearing nothing but a diaper went running by, chased by a slightly smaller child, who at least had a shirt on. Andrew watched them, and then he saw Gus, who had an even more intense look on his face if that were possible, and there was no doubt he adored his children.

Something else Lynette had left him, but he wouldn't have had if he hadn't given his heart.

Gus turned back to Andrew. "I'll have your cradle ready by Christmas Eve. I'll be going to the service that evening, so pick it up before that."

Andrew jerked his head. "Tell me what I owe you."

"No charge. Whatever your situation, I love that you're taking care of the mother of your child. Every woman should be so blessed to have a man who cares about her."

Gus completely misunderstood, but Andrew didn't correct him; he just said thanks and walked out. Somehow, through all of that, a phrase had popped into his head and wouldn't leave: death makes life worth living.

———

REAGAN ADJUSTED the bag with Dylan's costume in it in her hand and called up the stairs, "Dylan. Are you ready? We need to leave in the next five minutes in order for you to be there on time."

"Coming, Ray," Dylan's voice called down.

The front door burst open, and Andrew came in, dripping on the rug. "I brought the pickup as close as I can to the porch. It is pouring. Hopefully you guys don't mind getting a little bit wet."

"I don't think any of us will get upset if we get a few raindrops on us." Reagan watched as the rain dripped off his cowboy hat and onto the rug.

He'd changed a little in the last week, seeming to be more considerate, although he'd worked a forty-eight-hour shift in order to be off to go to Dylan's school play tonight, and she hadn't seen him much.

Not that Dylan had a huge part. He said one line, as part of the crowd in Charles Dickens's *A Christmas Carol*.

Regardless, it was one of her favorite Christmas stories, beyond the birth of Christ, and she was looking forward to seeing it. Even if it was a junior high production.

"I'm soaking wet. Would you mind checking Gladys in her cage one last time?" Andrew asked, just a thread of worry in his voice.

They hadn't left her alone at all since she'd had her operation. This was the first time that they were going anywhere without taking her with them. Uncle Ron had even stayed home from church on Sunday while Andrew worked, and Reagan took Dylan by herself.

"Sure." She turned to walk back to the kitchen.

"Reagan?"

She stopped and turned.

"I was hoping I could talk to you this evening maybe after everyone goes to bed?" he asked softly, probably making sure his voice didn't carry upstairs.

Her stomach twisted.

Surely he wasn't going to tell her that he wanted her to move out? Maybe he was going to insist she sign a lease. Maybe he was going to say something about the decorations she'd been putting up.

She took a deep breath and straightened her spine. "Of course."

She put a hand on her stomach. She did find more and more that any time life threw situations at her that she didn't particularly like, she wanted to protect her child from them. Even though she wasn't even born yet.

As she turned, Dylan came racing downstairs. "Are we stopping for ice cream at the all-night diner like we do every year?"

Reagan popped her head in the kitchen and checked Gladys in her cage. The dog whined and was not lying down, but she looked fine.

"No," she said to her brother as she walked back down the hall.

"But I bought ice cream and sundae toppings and some special sundae bowls, and I thought we could make our own sundaes this evening. It will be just as nice, and that way Gladys won't be here alone as long."

"If you guys want to go ahead and go to the diner, it's fine. You'll have to drive a separate vehicle." Andrew spoke and said the right words, but he didn't sound like that was what he wanted them to do. She was pretty sure with all the rain they'd gotten and with some roads already closed from the flooding, he wanted to drive them himself.

Nevertheless, she appreciated him being willing to not interrupt their tradition.

"No." She ignored the shadow on Dylan's face. True, it was one of the few traditions they had, but she wasn't going to sacrifice Gladys's well-being to it. "We're coming straight home this year. Next year will be a different story. Although, homemade sundaes might be a better tradition than stopping at the diner, since we can make them however we want to and put as much hot fudge on them as we feel like. I bought two jars."

"Cool! Seriously? I can put as much hot fudge on as I want?"

"You sure can. I also bought cookie dough and miniature chocolate candies. Your two favorites. Plus, I got a jar of maraschino cherries for me." She gave an apologetic glance at Uncle Ron. "I'm sorry. When I was in the store, I thought of asking you what your favorite toppings were, but you didn't answer your phone."

"You didn't ask me." Andrew crossed his arms over his chest, and there was more than a little pout in his voice. Mostly fake, she assumed.

"I did you one better. I asked Athena. She said you are a caramel and marshmallow cream guy." She laughed a little, remembering the total at the store. "I think it might be cheaper for us to go to the diner, but I still think it will be more fun to do it here."

Andrew grinned. "I can reimburse you for that." He'd been giving her grocery money, which she'd been giving back to him, and they'd been kind of having a bit of an argument over it. A passive argument, passive aggressive maybe. Although she was pretty sure it was in fun.

Once the total added up to a significant amount, maybe they'd all end up going somewhere together. She wasn't doing it to be unkind, and she didn't think he was either. But both of them seemed to be a little bit on the stubborn side.

They all made it out to the pickup without getting completely soaked, and Reagan enjoyed her evening sitting between Uncle Ron and Andrew.

Somehow Andrew looked at her and made her forget that she was getting ready to have a baby any day. Which she supposed should be weird, but it made for an enjoyable evening. Not that she wanted to forget about her baby, exactly, just that sometimes it was nice just to be with someone and enjoy their company.

Although every once in a while, she caught a look from Andrew that made her shiver.

Especially when she remembered that he wanted to talk to her later.

Hopefully it wasn't anything bad.

They got home and immediately. Gladys couldn't press herself against all of them tight enough, but especially Andrew.

He waited for a break in the rain showers before taking her outside, while Reagan got the ice cream out and set the toppings around the table along with the special bowls she'd bought.

Hopefully this was just as nice of a treat for Dylan as hanging out at the diner.

This was also the first year that their brothers hadn't made it, but they'd been going down to Texas to help someone they'd met winterize the pastures of a ranch they'd just bought. They'd said something about trading work and had sounded apologetic when they said they wouldn't be back for Christmas.

Reagan was disappointed, but she would never tell them that and insisted it was fine.

She didn't want them not to be able to live their dreams because they felt guilty, like they needed to take care of their family.

She was big enough to take care of herself, and she'd been doing a pretty good job of taking care of Dylan too. And she'd take care of this baby as well.

"What are you naming the baby?" Andrew asked as he walked in the back door, Gladys trailing behind him, the towel he'd used to try to dry her off some tossed in the hamper before he came through the door.

Her eyes fluttered in surprise. They hadn't talked about her baby for a while, and she assumed he was probably uninterested.

Maybe he was just making conversation, although he'd seemed quiet and pensive all week, and this seemed an odd subject to pick up when he finally did start talking again.

Regardless, she went with it.

"The ultrasound indicated I'm having a girl. I'm naming her Esme. On the off chance that it was wrong, I figured I ought to have a boy's name picked out, but I just don't." She shrugged. "I'll figure something out."

She'd love to have had someone to talk to about it. But that just hadn't worked out for her. She tried to want what she had, instead of what she didn't.

"I like Levi," Andrew said, like this was a completely normal subject for them to be talking about. "I had a buddy named Stetson when I went to fire school, thought that was a pretty cool name." He turned the faucet off and shook his hands in the sink before drying them on a towel. "I guess if I had another kid, I'd want to name him Shane."

That was all he said about it, and he didn't seem overly upset. Reagan narrowed her eyes at his back. Was he as unaffected as what he appeared to be?

He turned before she got the considering look off her face, and he grinned a little. "Surprised?"

"No, makes total sense to me that you'd want to name him that. I guess I'm just wondering if you're okay talking about it. I got the feeling it bothered you." To say the least.

Uncle Ron and Dylan were having some kind of animated conversation upstairs, and their voices drifted down. Reagan dug in the drawer for the ice-cream scooper and tried to be casual. Maybe she'd said too much.

"Just been doing some thinking. I suppose I've come to some conclusions, partly because of some things you said to me. I appreciate you being honest."

Her fingers paused in the drawer. She felt him behind her, then his hand landed on the counter beside her. "I needed someone to talk to me the way you did."

Her breath caught. She couldn't move away, because her stomach was already pressing against the drawer. She wasn't used to feeling this ungainly and wide. She wasn't used to wanting to get away from people but not being able to.

She didn't exactly want to get away, but she did feel...pressured.

"I wanted to thank you," he said softly.

He smelled like wind and rain along with the lingering spice of his aftershave, not overwhelming but deliciously good, and she breathed through her nose, wishing she could do what she wanted, which was turn around and touch him, maybe slide her hands over his shoulders and around his back and smile up into his face, and talk about baby names and friends and how they could pick up the pieces of their lives and move on, together.

Or maybe they could just pretend they were a family, Uncle Ron and Dylan and Andrew and her, and the baby between them.

Life was full of fantasies that would never happen.

There were footsteps on the stairs, and she almost didn't hear Andrew as he spoke low. "Are you still willing to talk to me later?"

She took another breath deep into her lungs before she nodded. She'd talk to him. And she'd face whatever it was he needed to say to her.

Chapter Fifteen

"Maybe we could walk outside?" Andrew asked, his stomach twisting and his fingers shaking, and he wasn't even sure why. Except maybe he thought Reagan would not only turn him down but would reject the idea that he'd been tossing around.

She talked about being brave. Not even that much, but she'd only needed to mention it for it to strike a chord in his heart.

He'd considered himself brave. He would never have said that he wasn't.

But she'd been right. Maybe he was brave when it came to physical danger, but for the things he wanted to do tonight? Not so much.

He could face a rock wall with nothing more than climbing shoes and a couple of ropes with less trepidation than he faced the woman walking down the stairs.

"Did it stop raining?" she asked softly.

"We're between showers. The way the radar looks, it'll be a couple of hours until the next one. I thought you might want to walk down the road and stand on the bridge. The water's pretty high, and it's amazing to stand over all that power."

He felt stupid after he said it. It probably wasn't something that she'd be interested in. Somehow, it just thrilled him and challenged him at the same time to see the floodwaters raging, not that he wanted to pit himself against them exactly, but it inspired an amazement and a feeling of smallness, next to all that power, but also he felt a challenge deep in his soul he couldn't explain but that fascinated him.

He could stand and watch the river at flood stage for hours.

It was a stupid place to ask her to go with him. But the words were out there.

"I'd love to." She came to the bottom of the stairs, and he probably should've backed up to give her room to get through, but he didn't. "I need to get my jacket," she whispered softly.

"I'll wait here."

She moved by him, her arm brushing his stomach as she went by. He breathed her sweet vanilla and flowers scent, unable to place a finger exactly on what it was that it reminded him of, other than a soft toughness, which was the way she seemed to live her life.

Maybe he'd be able to figure out how to tell her he admired her tonight.

His eyes followed her as she walked down the dim hall, the shimmer of her hair, the slenderness of her back, even the curve of her stomach and the slightly off-center wobble to her walk.

Her shoulders were back, and she walked the way she lived, with as much grace and strength as anyone could expect.

She came back, and he opened the door. She walked by with him breathing deep and allowing Gladys to go through as well before he stepped through and closed the door behind him.

Once before he held her hand, and he hoped she was okay as his fingers touched hers before sliding around and entwining them together. They stepped off the porch steps side by side.

She didn't resist, and he took that as acceptance, if not eagerness.

They moseyed out the drive, neither one of them saying anything, and turned right where the drive met paved road. It was a quarter-mile walk and not something they could see from the house.

He wished everything he wanted to say would come out without him having to breathe a word. He enjoyed the silence, it felt companionable to him, and he enjoyed the movement of the woman beside him. He didn't want to ruin it by talking about things that he felt he needed to.

Maybe he could start with the easiest thing first. "I spoke with Preston yesterday."

"How's he doing?" Reagan asked, and if there was any lingering anger or bitterness in her heart over him showing up sauced on Thanksgiving, he couldn't detect it in her tone.

"Same. But I got a promise out of him."

"What's that?"

"I know you're due on Christmas Eve, which is less than a week away. Just in case I'm taking you to the hospital on Christmas. I didn't want Dylan here spending Christmas by himself with Uncle Ron. Preston's on call to make sure that Dylan and Uncle Ron have a good time on Christmas in case you're in the hospital. I just wanted you to know."

They took about five steps with her not saying a word, which made his stomach clench even tighter. He probably should have asked her first, but he thought he was doing a good thing, and it hadn't really occurred to him.

"It sounds like...you're planning on being at the hospital with me?"

It was his turn to walk in silence. He just assumed he was going to the hospital with her. "Did you have someone else?" He knew she wasn't going to have the father of the baby there. And while she had friends in town, Violet and others, he hadn't seen her talking with anyone, and she hadn't mentioned anyone. Feeling like maybe he'd just made a huge blunder, he held his breath and waited.

"No. I don't. I hadn't wanted to ask anyone, in case it did happen on Christmas or Christmas Eve. I didn't want anyone to miss the holiday with their family."

"Well, I'm already planning on being with you, so I'm not missing anything." There was a lot in those words, some that maybe he didn't exactly want her to hear, although he was planning on saying that a lot more tonight, if he didn't let his fear control him.

He took a deep breath. "Is that okay?"

Please say yes. Please say yes.

"I guess you have no idea how much that eases my mind. I was a little scared to go by myself."

Thankful for the darkness and the cloud cover that kept her from seeing the widening of his eyes and the clenching of his jaw, he tried to stay calm.

He hadn't been planning on going into the delivery room with her. He figured he'd stay in the waiting room.

Fear backed up his throat and stiffened his neck and made his stomach fold over again and again, but he couldn't say anything and couldn't figure out how to word the question that would clarify everything.

Maybe there were some other things he needed to talk about first.

"I told you I'd been thinking about what you said to me."

"Yes?"

"I've been thinking about a few more things too."

"And?"

"Things that have to do with you, and I wanted to talk to you a bit about them."

"So you're not kicking me out?"

"No! Of course not. Probably the exact opposite of that." How could she even think that?

"You want me to sign a long-term lease?"

"No. No, nothing to have to do with you renting anything..." His voice trailed off; he'd bungled this badly.

Marshaling his thoughts together, he tried to be clear. "I guess you probably already know that I like you. A lot. I guess you probably know, too, that I'm attracted to you, and while I know it's probably not the smartest thing that you've ever done to walk alone in the dark with me, letting me hold your hand and be beside you, I assume, since you're allowing it, especially this," he held up their joined hands, "that maybe you're okay with it?"

"Yes."

"I want more."

The river had been rumbling for a while, and it got louder as they got closer, and as they reached the bridge, they could feel the slight shaking of the ground as the water thundered past. They walked a few feet out on the bridge before he tugged on her hand, and they leaned against the cement edge, which was chest height for her and slightly lower for him. There wasn't much light to reflect off the water, but they didn't need it. Somehow the dark maybe made it more menacing, with an occasional gleaming glisten as the water roiled and fought beneath them.

"More?" She turned her head to look at him.

"Yes." His eyes ran over the outline of her features, unable to read anything in her expression, but he reminded himself to be brave.

It was easier to be brave if he was looking at the water, strong and fierce and unafraid.

It had to be enough to feel it. His hand tightened around hers. "I want to be more than friends. I want to be the only one who walks beside you. I want to help you with the baby. I want to be someone you can depend on."

All those statements felt scary. He wanted far more than that, but he didn't want to ask for more than she was ready to give.

The water thundered by, and his hand started to sweat, but he didn't want to pull it away from hers, didn't want to lose the link between them, didn't want to hear her rejection, but he held himself still, determined to see it through.

"I wanted that too. All of it."

Her words eased some of the tightness in his chest, but he could almost hear the "but" she hadn't spoken. He waited.

"I suppose, though, it scares me that you had such an addiction to danger and the rush of adrenaline, and maybe I'm a little scared that it will be something you want to do again once you get over Shane's death and move on. And life is fragile enough. I don't want to lose the person I'm depending on, because he's seeking out the next adrenaline high."

She shifted, although she didn't pull her hand away, but she turned to completely face him. "Even your choice tonight...standing here on the bridge, I could feel the change in you when we only started to hear the water. I can feel it now. You can't tell me that the rushing water doesn't call you at some kind of elemental level. Not that you would do something stupid, necessarily, but there's a pull there. Something I don't understand." She shifted her feet. "Am I wrong?"

He couldn't deny it. She was absolutely right. He had thought it made him a better person. But looking at it through her eyes, he could understand the concern. She had a baby to think of. She didn't want the child to get attached to someone who was going to decide in ten years to go climb Mount Everest, walk off into the mist and snow, never to return.

If she pressed him, he could never deny the fact that in the back of his head, yeah, he'd never pass up the opportunity to climb the world's highest mountain; it was a challenge that spoke to him. Like a lot of other things.

Oh, but she wasn't done with him. "You can't tell me that you are thinking about pulling your fields out of the rental agreement, becoming a rancher?"

It didn't take a rocket scientist to hear the hope in her voice. She wanted him to be a farmer, rancher, cowboy. It was his heritage.

There was a part of him that wanted that too. But he had to be honest.

"That's never going to be me. I might pull my fields out, I might farm them myself, but that's never going to be the bulk of who I am."

"I didn't think so." She turned back to the bridge and put her free hand on the top of the cement side, leaning into the cement and putting her head over like she was studying the water, although she couldn't see but mere glimpses of it.

"I think there's been a change in you. But I can't put my finger on it. It's like you stepped out of the darkness that was holding you fast, and I think it was because of Shane's death." She looked back over her shoulder to him. "There's something different about you."

There was. He'd made peace with death. Not his death, but the people around him.

He'd internalized what Gus had said, what Reagan had paved the way toward with her probing questions—that life without love wasn't a worthwhile life. He couldn't keep from facing death, from losing to death, but he'd been struck by the realization that he had to love, had to give it away to make it worth something, had to take the chance and live the risk, in order to make his life worthwhile.

Death was inevitable. For him and everyone else. But he couldn't live his life afraid. In order to make his life worth living, worth dying for, he had to live and love, unafraid.

Gus hadn't preached to him, but he hadn't needed to.

Andrew had heard plenty of sermons over his lifetime, but the words that Gus had said had been enough.

He didn't have words to tell Reagan how he felt, and he was pretty sure she'd rejected him anyway.

He turned his body and leaned against the cement, the hand that wasn't holding hers resting on the top of it as he leaned over as well.

Gus had sent him a link after he'd left his barn, a link with the story of a man who had lost his four daughters in a tragic accident and then written a song that was so divinely beautiful that it couldn't help but touch Andrew's heart and make sense of the loss of his friend.

Maybe he didn't have words, not words to explain, but he had a song.

He couldn't talk to Reagan, but he could sing with her.

When peace like a river attendeth my way
When sorrows like sea billows roll;
Whatever my lot, Thou hast taught me to say
It is well, it is well with my soul.
Though Satan should buffet, though trials should come,
Let this blest assurance control,
That Christ has regarded my helpless estate,
And has shed His own blood for my soul.
It is well (it is well)
With my soul (with my soul)
It is well, it is well with my soul.
My sin, oh, the bliss of this glorious thought!
My sin, not in part but the whole,
Is nailed to the cross, and I bear it no more,
Praise the Lord, praise the Lord, O my soul!
And, Lord, haste the day, when the faith shall be sight,
The clouds be rolled back as a scroll;
The trump shall resound, and the Lord shall descend,
Even so, it is well with my soul.

It is well (it is well)
With my soul (with my soul)
It is well, it is well with my soul.

Chapter Sixteen

The last notes of the song faded away, and Reagan stood with her hand in Andrew's, part fear, part excitement duking it out in her chest.

"I've always loved that song," she said softly.

"I loved having you sing with me," he said, just as low and soft.

There was no doubt the song was calming.

She could understand the deep emotions that the powerful floodwaters elicited in Andrew. They did the same for her, in a way.

They didn't inspire her to want to conquer or subdue or make her feel challenged to rise and war.

She was grateful for his hand holding hers. She would have been even more grateful for his arm around her and to be tucked a little closer beside him.

His desire to take risks, to prove his mettle against nature, wasn't really something she understood, but she could appreciate having a man beside her that she was confident would protect her and keep her safe.

There was definitely something very appealing about that.

But on the flipside, there was something that was almost repelling about being with someone who took his own safety so lightly and who would risk his very life for something so transient and unimportant.

Not that she thought he was going to jump off the bridge or that he'd even consider it. But if there was a need to go in the water, she knew he wouldn't hesitate.

She admired it and feared it at the same time.

She put her hand over her stomach. She had her own form of protection to do, and as much as she enjoyed standing with Andrew on the bridge, she felt slightly unsafe and itchy which caused her to be restless, like she needed to get off.

Her hand tightened.

That seemed to startle him out of whatever reverie he'd been in, and he looked down at her like he'd forgotten she was beside him.

"I'm sorry," he said. "We've stood here long enough. I didn't mean to be inconsiderate. I could spend hours here."

"You're not being inconsiderate. And I can understand the draw. I feel it too. Definitely not as strong, I'm sure. And mixed with that pull is enough fear to make me very uncomfortable."

He stopped turning and seemed to consider her words. After a moment of consideration, he loosened his hand from hers and slid his arm around her shoulders, pulling her in closer and tucking her shoulder under his armpit.

"Better?" he asked.

There was no arrogance or even humor in his voice, although she would have understood the origins of both. But it was more just a soft desire to ease her fear.

It was the protector in him.

Maybe there was just something about singing together that made her feel more at ease with him. Or closer to him.

Not a physical closeness, but a mental or maybe spiritual closeness. It was odd, but it didn't feel weird to put her arm around him and tuck her body next to his, her stomach pressed against his and his arm holding her close.

"Much better," she murmured against him.

"You have to know this is everything I want and more than I deserve."

His words stirred the same fear they had earlier. He could leave and never come back. His job was dangerous, and he wasn't the kind of man to sit on the sidelines and let someone else take the risk. That's why he was the chief, and she knew he'd lead from the front, and he would take the most dangerous position for himself.

She wasn't typically afraid; even though her parents had left, and her older brothers, and she hadn't had much stability in her life at all, she'd not been scared to love people.

But this was completely different. It wasn't a fear that he would leave her or hurt her or cheat on her; he just wasn't that kind of man, and that would never happen.

"I scared you, didn't I?" There was a rueful resignation in his tone.

"A little," she said honestly. "Not necessarily in a bad way. Just, I know you're not going to protect yourself, and you're going to take on the danger, and while I'm not afraid of the normal issues, trust issues maybe, I don't want to constantly worry about whether or not you're coming home."

She said maybe more than she should. He wasn't talking about a long-term relationship, and she was. She didn't really go into any relationships thinking they were just a fling. She always thought long-term. Even with Dr. Michael, she'd been thinking long-term. He was the one that was thinking fling.

"I suppose after what your last boyfriend did to you, it's probably hard to trust again."

His hand moved up and down her arm, and she nestled her head more snugly against him.

"It's honestly not that. You'd think it would be. Him, my mom, my dad, even my brothers all left. You'd think I'd have gotten smart a long time ago, but I'm not afraid to trust people. And, knowing you, I'm definitely not afraid, because I know you're going to do exactly what you say you're going to."

"You know you never told me about him."

"I can."

"Don't. Not if you don't want to."

"I worked at the vet clinic in Trumbull. His vet clinic. He'd sit around over lunch on my desk and complain to me about his wife. Eventually he said he left her. They were separated and getting divorced. In hindsight, I should have waited until he said the divorce was final, but I guess he could have lied about that, too, and I believed everything he said. When he asked me out, I went. I was just in over my head; he was a lot older than I was, and I wasn't expecting things to move as quickly as they did. I guess maybe I was a little afraid to tell him no, but I can't blame him, because I definitely wasn't forced or anything like that. I knew exactly what I was doing. And it's funny, even at the time, I knew I was being stupid. But I didn't want to lose my job, and I didn't want to lose a man that I thought was a really good catch, and yeah, I'm just as dumb as every other woman who's done the exact same things, and I should've known better, but it's funny how furiously you can love someone that you've never even met." She put a hand on her stomach.

"You told him about the baby?"

"Yeah. I did. And right after I told him about the baby, he told me his wife and he were working things out. He did offer to pay for me to go down to the clinic. Get rid of this 'problem.' When I refused, he tried to make me sign some papers from his lawyer releasing him from any parental responsibility. I quit the day he gave them to me."

"You didn't sign them?"

"No. But I don't want anything from him anyway. I just didn't want to be forced into it. I guess I just kind of feel like money doesn't make him a father. And he's right, although I don't want to have papers between us saying so, but I'm choosing to have the baby and keep her, and at the very least, he'd want me to give her up for adoption. I don't want to force him into sending money to something he doesn't want. Maybe that doesn't make sense."

"I can see it. I know I've never really heard that before, but I can see what you're saying. I understand your point, and I admire you for being fair to someone who wasn't fair to you."

"Maybe if I had more feelings for him, it might hurt more, but honestly, the guy was a jerk. All he did was talk about himself on our date, and the evening didn't get any better from there. Which just makes me stupider, but I suppose I'll be smarter next time."

"Maybe there won't be a next time."

She laughed without humor. "Hopefully not a next time with someone like him. But I do want to get married and have a family sometime. A real family, not the kind that I came from. Like with a mom and a dad at the supper table together, and kids they raise together, and a family vacation, even if it's just camping at the state park. Just family stuff. I've always wanted that. Like what we did on Thanksgiving. It wasn't hard to imagine I was part of a family, and we were doing the fun things I've always wanted to."

"I guess I take my upbringing on the farm for granted. We did the family thing, and I didn't appreciate it. I couldn't wait to get away. Couldn't wait to do something more challenging, something exciting and fun, something that didn't involve getting up with the crack of dawn and working all day long and dropping into bed at night and falling asleep without moving because you're just too stinking tired. That didn't seem like a life to me. And I couldn't wait to get away."

"Maybe it depends on your attitude. Or on who you're sharing it with."

"Maybe. There's just something inside of me that needs to be challenged that just gets scared at even the thought of day in, day out, everything the same, no danger, no excitement, no fun."

Her heart hurt a little at that, because that could be marriage. Day in, day out, everything exactly the same, not the challenge of a new love, but the same one all the time. A man like Andrew would find that boring.

When she didn't say anything, he squeezed her shoulders. "What? What did I say?"

"I was just thinking you were making an argument against

marriage. Because isn't that what it is? You settled the challenge. It's the same, day in, day out, with the same person, nothing new or challenging or exciting."

Maybe she shouldn't have said that. They weren't talking about marriage. They weren't even talking about a long-term relationship, other than him helping her with her baby. She was way ahead of everything. But that's just where her mind went.

"I think that's different," he finally said.

"I guess I don't see how."

"Maybe the challenge in marriage is fighting against everything that you just said. Fighting against the idea that there is something more exciting somewhere else. Fighting against the idea that it's boring and you want to quit. The challenge in marriage is the daily fight to do right. That can't be boring."

"I'm sorry. I guess that's a way to look at it. But from what you were saying earlier, about living on the farm, I guess I just assumed you'd apply that to marriage as well."

"I don't even know if I feel that way about living on the farm anymore. I kind of was getting a hankering there this fall to put some seeds in the ground and see if I can't coax a little something from it. There's a challenge there too. I guess when I was younger, I just didn't see it. Or maybe it wasn't exciting enough. But now that I've seen where the excitement I was after leads—it's just an empty glory—maybe there's something a little more substantial to what I had originally dismissed as old-fashioned and only something for people who are uninspired and unmotivated to look for the real excitement and meaning of life."

"That's a little harsh."

"I was young and dumb once too. Not that young anymore, but I think I'm still dumb sometimes."

"We've got that in common anyway."

He took a hold of her shoulders, held her away from him, and looked down at her. "I don't think you're dumb. You made a mistake. I admire the way you're taking responsibility for what you've done and how you're handling it. How can I not admire that? You're strong and smart and willing to sacrifice to give others everything you can. That's not dumb."

"I guess we have some more things in common," she said softly.

She thought maybe he wasn't going to answer her, but then he finally said, "Maybe we do."

They stood there for just a few moments. She thought maybe he'd kiss her, and even more surprisingly, she thought she'd let him.

But he didn't, just turned her, took her hand, and started walking home.

Chapter Seventeen

"Merry Christmas Eve, beautiful," Andrew said with a grin as he walked in the front door with Gladys and saw Reagan coming down the steps, one hand on her stomach, one hand on the banister. She walked a little unevenly, like maybe her back was sore.

He'd asked her about it, but she'd been finding it more and more difficult to get comfortable in any position, and there wasn't really anything he could do about it.

She was still beautiful, smiling, her eyes still a little sleepy, and her cheeks rosy and deepening in color at his words.

He loved that he could compliment her and she didn't brush it off, didn't act like she deserved it, but just seemed to appreciate it. Made him want to say more.

He closed the door and stood on the rug with Gladys beside him, waiting for the worst of the rain to drip off.

"It's still raining?" she asked incredulously. "I thought we saw on the weather yesterday that it was going to stop. Finally."

"That's what they said. But there's no doubt there's water falling from the sky."

"This has to be the wettest year on record. At least the wettest December on record."

"Sure is. It's rained every day this month."

"It'd be fun to get a little snow today." She grinned. "And Merry Christmas Eve to you too."

"I suppose, since tomorrow is Christmas, I won't get upset with you for saying the 's' word in my house. But don't think for one second that you are going to get away with it next week this time."

She laughed and finished coming downstairs.

"Back hurt?" he asked.

"Same old, same old," she said. "She's moved around quite a bit today though, so she's in good shape. Would you like waffles for breakfast? Do you have a tradition you do on Christmas Eve?" She laughed a little. "I probably should have asked earlier. I might not have all the ingredients if you have something really special you do."

"No tradition. Just always go to the candlelight service in the evening. I really love it."

"Me too. My favorite service. I look forward to it." She stopped in front of him, not too close. She probably didn't mean anything by it, but his hands came up and landed on her upper arms, and he started to lean in.

He was wet and dripping on her. He shouldn't even be touching her, but she didn't say anything. In fact, he didn't think he was imagining her leaning closer, and he definitely wasn't imagining her arms landing on his chest and moving up.

Warning bells went off in his head, and he knew after everything she'd gone through, he shouldn't kiss her without some kind of guarantee from him to assure her he meant it and it wasn't just a onetime deal. She didn't deserve less.

She deserved a whole lot more.

The idea made him freeze for a moment. Could he give her more?

He already knew he wanted to. But could he?

She was complicated. She came with a baby and a brother...of course he wasn't exactly uncomplicated, coming with Uncle Ron and a whole lot of baggage. Although she'd kinda been helping him work through that baggage, and he felt a lot lighter than he had in a long time.

Although his conversation on the phone with Preston last night had been depressing.

He came with Uncle Ron and a friend who had a major problem with alcohol and denial.

Maybe they could take a chance on each other.

Her face had twitched and tightened just a little as he stopped and leaned forward, opening his mouth to ask her if she was willing to take a chance on him and to offer her whatever long-term commitment she wanted.

But he didn't get the chance, because Dylan came skipping down the steps. "It's Christmas Eve! It's Christmas Eve! Are we opening any presents today? I think I get to open one. And, Reagan, I need wrapping paper. And I couldn't find the tape yesterday either. And can we finish decorating the tree?"

Andrew brushed his thumb over her cheek and down her chin, exchanging a rueful grin with her.

"I think I'm falling for you, but I'm not sure how I feel about your brother right now," he said, meaning to be flippant, knowing that he cracked his heart open just a little for her.

Her mouth pursed, and surprise crossed her features, but before she could say anything, Uncle Ron appeared at the top of the steps, wearing the ugliest Christmas sweater Andrew had ever seen and speaking before Reagan had a chance.

"You couldn't find the tape, Dylan, because I have it. You're not the only one that has gifts to wrap. And if you want to finish decorating the tree, we need to go to the attic and find that last box of decorations. I'm not sure what Andrew did with that, but it's gotta be around here somewhere. We just have to search for it."

"If we can't find it, I could probably bake some gingerbread cookies that we could decorate and hang on the tree instead. I've got some ribbon, and I'm pretty sure we have enough paint to at least put faces on them," Reagan said as she moved away from him and Andrew's hand slipped off her shoulder and fell down to his side.

Now wasn't the time, and he shouldn't have said what he did, but he wished he could just take her somewhere and hold her and kiss her and make sure that they both wanted the same things—most notably a long-term relationship and a full commitment.

He was pretty sure he was ready to give both of those, and he hoped she was too.

Gladys wasn't completely dry, but he figured she was good enough, and they followed Reagan and Uncle Ron and Dylan into the kitchen.

"How do waffles for breakfast sound?" Reagan asked.

"I thought we're making gingerbread men for the Christmas tree?" Dylan asked.

"We're going to go up to the attic to look for those ornaments first," Uncle Ron said.

Reagan was looking a little overwhelmed, and Andrew was going to step in and bring some order to the situation, when his phone buzzed and he pulled it out.

It was a text from the station. He read it quickly.

Reagan must have been watching his face and could probably tell it wasn't good news, because as soon as his eyes stopped moving, she said, "What is it?"

Her hand went to her chest, and her brows drew down.

Maybe, if they were together long enough, she would get used to him being called out for accidents and more, or maybe it was something a person never got used to.

What a day for a catastrophe. He dropped his hand and looked up at her. "There was a mudslide on Route 23, right there as you're going up the side of the mountain. There was a wildfire there a year or so ago. Last summer. Anyway, it washed the road out or at least covered it. They're going to try to dig through and open it back up since there's no other good way around the mountain. But more concerning is they think several cars were caught in the mudslide and swept down the mountain. I need to go."

His head was already out of the kitchen and at the fire station, thinking of the things he needed to do and the things he might be facing.

He turned and had taken two steps before he realized that maybe he ought to leave with a little bit more emotion.

He spun around and strode directly back to Reagan, shoving his hand in the hair at the back of her head, bending over, pressing his lips to hers, and wrapping his other arm around her back.

Maybe it wasn't the smartest move he'd ever made, because he hadn't meant for it to be a long kiss. Just wanted to do more than walk away from her without letting her know how he felt.

Which wasn't the easiest thing for him to do to begin with, and he'd been spending days trying to figure out exactly how, and now he needed to leave and was out of time.

Regardless, the quick kiss he'd planned, on the spur of the moment, deepened into more as her breath hitched and her body shuddered and his heart shuddered with it and his fingers curled, and for the first time in his life, the idea of excitement and adventure wasn't enough to get his feet moving, and he needed to dredge up the sense of duty and responsibility to make himself pull away.

But he did let go, and they stared at each other, her eyes clouded with passion and overshadowed with fear, her brows drawn with worry, her lips swollen but pressed together, and her fingers tightening on him.

"If you're going to go, boy, you need to get out of here. There are people who need you." Uncle Ron's voice came from what felt like far away but was only a few feet. Even Dylan was quiet for once.

He'd kissed her under the mistletoe and left like it didn't mean anything. And here he was, doing it again.

Surely this time she knew it did. Surely she knew he wouldn't have walked back and kissed her without a very good reason and without any meaning behind it. He could have kept walking. Surely she knew what it meant.

But maybe she didn't.

And how was he supposed to tell her? He didn't even know. He just knew he'd never wanted to stay before.

"I know, Uncle Ron. I'm leaving." He spoke without taking his eyes off her, hoping that beyond the passion and fear, understanding would sweep through, but as the passion faded, fear and worry just took over.

He tore his eyes away. He had a job to do; people were depending on him. She'd just have to wait 'til he got back. The first thing he would do would be to sit down and explain everything to her.

Lay it all out. And offer her...offer her his heart.

He supposed, if he were very, very blessed, she'd offer hers in return.

And then they could figure everything else out.

———

By 6 o'clock that evening, Andrew still wasn't home.

Reagan was in her room, getting dressed for the Christmas Eve service and wishing she could take some kind of pain medicine for the terrible backache she'd had all day. It made sense that this late in her pregnancy it would be the worst backache she'd ever had.

Felt like someone had lit her back on fire and was standing there with the blowtorch fanning the flames.

She wasn't quite sure how she was going to sit through the service tonight. The pews weren't padded.

But she didn't care about that, if Andrew would just come home.

Common sense told her they wouldn't have the firefighters digging through the mudslide, and they wouldn't have anyone digging where they thought there might be another one, but she also knew that if they were looking for volunteers, Andrew would be the first to step forward.

She loved that about him.

She hated it too.

No, that wasn't really true. She didn't hate it. She just hated the idea.

She bit her lip and pulled the one maternity shirt she had out of her closet and grabbed the serviceable black skirt that she'd been wearing her entire pregnancy. Being pregnant had definitely narrowed down her choices and streamlined her getting ready process.

When one had one shirt and one skirt that fit, it didn't take long to decide what to wear.

And it didn't do anything to take her mind off Andrew and what he might be doing.

She hadn't tried to text him or even call, because she didn't want to distract him from whatever job he was doing.

She did try to look at the news but didn't find anything but perfunctory information: The road was closed, they were working on opening it, two cars had disappeared in the mudslide, and crews were working to recover anyone who might still be alive.

"Reagan? Is Mr. Andrew going to be home in time to go with us?" Dylan's voice came through her door.

She wanted to snap back, like how was she supposed to know? But he was a kid, and he thought she had all the answers.

She heard Uncle Ron's voice murmuring to him, and she assumed Uncle Ron was explaining that she wouldn't know. But she'd taken long enough to get ready, and they might as well leave.

With both hands on her back, she stretched and tried to pull out the kink or whatever it was that was making her back hurt so bad, but her midsection tightened, painfully, which was kind of a good thing, because it hurt so bad it made her forget about her back.

Probably more Braxton Hicks contractions. She'd been having them on and off all day.

Although today was her due date.

But she couldn't be in labor because she should feel different than she'd been feeling, which was pretty miserable. It was hard to imagine she could feel even more miserable, but the thought was there, kind of encouraging that she wasn't feeling as miserable as she could feel.

Actually she would forget all about how miserable she was if Andrew would just walk in.

But he didn't, and they left for the service, her favorite one of the year. She didn't want to miss it, except it would've been fun to share it with Andrew, since he claimed it was his favorite as well.

The church was dark, with white Christmas lights lit all around, lending a beautiful and contemplative glow and turning the sanctuary into something new and different.

A beautiful night to reflect on the birth of a baby to strangers in a strange town.

Definitely this year, Reagan felt a much greater kinship with Mary and wondered at the fear she must've felt, alone and in pain, as Joseph helped deliver a child that wasn't his.

She'd never stopped to wonder before how Joseph might have felt. In her mind, she carried her baby for nine months, and she already loved her, so although Mary was probably in a great deal of pain and, if she were anything like Reagan, consumed with fear, once the baby was born, it would've been love and protection at first sight. For Mary.

But Joseph?

How did Joseph feel about the baby?

She wasn't sure exactly what the pastor said in his message, because she mulled that question over and over in her head.

Would she love a baby that wasn't hers?

Her gut said yes. Just one look at an innocent, helpless baby, and she wouldn't care whose it was.

But maybe that was her nature, maybe that was a female nature. She kind of thought it was human nature.

Who didn't love a puppy? Or kitten? Or any baby animal?

The feelings were multiplied with a baby human. Except...were they?

The candles were lit, and the congregation softly sang "Silent Night."

Reagan joined in and thought about a few nights ago when Andrew stood on the bridge and sang "It is Well with My Soul."

He'd seemed to come to terms with the death of his friend and the fragility of life, and how loving makes life worth living, and how death reaffirms the importance of life.

But she wasn't sure what that meant for her.

Grateful for the chance to stand, she realized that not only was her back pain worse, but the tightening in her stomach had stopped being a mild annoyance and had made her want to stop breathing every time it happened during the service. Maybe three times.

That seemed like a lot for an hour.

She kept track in the back of her head as they drove home and grabbed some tuna salad sandwiches, and she made sure the turkey and potatoes and the other things she had for the meal that they were going to have tomorrow were out and ready for her to put together quickly in the morning. She double-checked the poundage on the turkey and calculated in her head how many hours it needed to cook. Everything was ready.

"I'm going to head upstairs to bed. It's a late night for an old man," Uncle Ron said, his gnarled hand landing lightly on her shoulder. "Andrew's done this a hundred times before. He'll be back. Don't you go and worry yourself over it. Promise me?"

"I won't." She didn't exactly promise, but she did say she wouldn't, which was basically the same thing. She hoped she could keep her word.

"I'm getting up at 4 o'clock in the morning," Dylan said.

"That's fine. If you get up at four, just know that you're gonna have about four hours before you see me."

"I don't have to wait for you, do I?" he asked eagerly, although he knew the answer, and all Reagan did was raise a brow, and his face fell.

"Don't forget to brush your teeth, kid."

"I think you care more about my teeth than you do about me," Dylan said, a little sullenly.

He turned to go, and despite the pain that was pushing around her back and banding in her front and slicing down her legs, she watched him go with a sad heart. No mom, no dad, only a sister who was half screwed up herself. Poor Dylan. She wanted to do so much better by him, but she only managed to mess everything up.

It'd been raining all evening, and it sounded like it was getting heavier, and because she knew she'd go upstairs and wouldn't be able to sleep anyway because of the pain in her back, she thought she'd go outside and sit on the swing and see if she could rock it away.

Three hours later, the rain had stopped, but her pain had not. It had gotten worse, and she was pretty sure this was the real deal.

She had to wait for the most recent contraction to pass before she could think about what to do. Tomorrow was Christmas. She couldn't just leave.

Could she drive herself in to the hospital and leave a note on the table where Uncle Ron would see it? She hated to leave without saying anything.

And also, Andrew had arranged with Preston to come, on the off chance that they wouldn't be here.

She reached for her phone but stopped and waited through another contraction. They seemed to be getting longer and closer together. Maybe she should start timing them?

They left her breathless and a little weak, but she reached again for a phone and searched through the contacts. Andrew had insisted he put Preston's number in her phone, and she'd argued with him at the time, never thinking that she'd need the friend who'd shown up drunk for Thanksgiving dinner, but she was glad for Andrew's provision now.

Hopefully he'd be awake. And sober. She couldn't ask him to drive over if he wasn't.

Christmas Eve. What were the odds?

She pulled it up but didn't hit the call button until she waited through another contraction.

Finally, she put the phone to her ear and waited while it rang.

He finally answered when she'd almost given up. "Hello?"

"Preston, this is Reagan, Andrew's friend?"

There were a few beats of silence while she worried her lip and hoped he figured it out.

"Reagan the pregnant lady?"

"Yeah. That's me."

Tomorrow this time, it wouldn't be her. She'd be holding her baby. She tried to hold onto that thought as new pain, sharper pain, cinched through her, and she bit down on the inside of her lips.

"Well? What do you want?" Preston didn't sound impatient, exactly, as much as exasperated. Like she'd called him and then just sat there.

He had no idea.

It was a few more seconds before she could get enough breath to talk. "I'm heading to the hospital," she said in her calmest tone. "Andrew said you'd be willing to come over and spend Christmas Day with Uncle Ron and Dylan if we couldn't be there."

"Why isn't Andrew calling me?"

"He was called out."

Hopefully this conversation ended soon...

Never mind. Another contraction made her hold her breath.

She needed to get herself to the hospital, quickly, before she couldn't drive.

"I'll be right over."

The pain receded enough for her to take two deep breaths and try to sound normal. "Thank you. I'm not going to wait. If there are any problems, please call me." She hung up before he could say anything else. All of the sudden in the last thirty seconds, she'd decided it was imperative that she get to the hospital. That new, sharper pain was scaring her, and she wasn't sure if it was normal.

She'd been told to expect pain, and lots of it, so it probably was, but she wasn't entirely sure.

As she ran to grab her bag and throw a note on the table, she thought again of Mary, alone and scared, with no one to reassure her that any new, sharper pain was normal or to help her if it wasn't.

She hoped Joseph was sympathetic and compassionate. She could use some of that herself right now.

Stopping to double over around a new contraction, she gathered the things in her room as softly as she could and headed down the stairs.

At the bottom, she had to double over again, and that's what she was doing when the door opened and Andrew walked in.

Chapter Eighteen

Andrew stared.

It took him at least a second to process exactly what was going on before he shoved Gladys aside and took the two steps to Reagan.

"Does this mean what I think it means?" He had some EMT training and in fact had taken several classes on emergency childbirth, but he certainly didn't want Reagan to be his first delivery.

Real life had a tendency to be nothing like the textbook version. Which, if he recalled correctly, was scary enough.

"Did you call an ambulance? Is someone coming to get you?" he asked, trying to keep the panic out of his voice. She was doubled over and wasn't moving. He wasn't even sure she was breathing.

Could a person pass out and remain upright?

"Talk to me. Reagan?" He hadn't stopped at the station on his way through, and he was still dressed in his fire gear, wet and muddy. He was about to put his arms around her anyway and lift her up when she slowly straightened.

"I'm sorry. The pain is too bad, and all I can do is just endure." She sounded breathless and tired.

"Has it been going all day?"

"Sort of. I've had a backache all day, and contractions off and on, but they didn't start getting stronger until just before we left for church. I'm not even sure what time it is. Six hours ago?"

"Let me call Preston, or Athena, and actually no...let's go out first...no, wait...I need to change...wait, no...I don't have time to change...actually, no...you're ready to go...let's just go—"

"Calm down," she said, putting a hand on his forearm. "We've got time."

She sounded relaxed, which did a lot toward easing the tight springs that had wound up in his chest and made him want to do something, anything, to take care of the situation.

But then she ruined it by adding, "I think."

He swore.

She flinched.

"Sorry."

She waved a hand.

"If you think I have a minute to change..."

"Go change. I already called Preston. Athena didn't answer."

"Be right back." He wanted to touch her, hold her, go to the hospital immediately, but it just made sense to change so he didn't get her wet and muddy.

It felt like forever, but it must've been only thirty seconds later when he came running back down the steps. His wet clothes were lying in a heap on the floor, but he didn't care.

"You ready?" He grabbed her bag and her hand, but she didn't move and slowly doubled over.

His heart raced, and his stomach churned, but this was what she had been doing when he walked in, and she survived that time.

She'd said her back hurt. He set the bag down and started carefully to rub it. But he'd barely touched her when she shook her head almost violently.

He jerked his hand back and just stared at her, his hands clenched, feeling helpless, like he needed to do something, anything.

He could hardly stand it until she slowly relaxed and straightened.

"I'm sorry. It hurts so much, even the light touch that you were doing, which normally would be wonderful, just felt supersensitive and painful. Sorry."

"Not your fault. Let's get you out to the truck between contractions. Come on." He couldn't get her to the hospital soon enough.

Of course, what in the world he was gonna do when they got there, he had no idea. He couldn't bear to just stand around and stare at her. No, what he couldn't stand was seeing her in pain and not being able to do anything about it.

Thankfully, she was in the truck and buckled before the next contraction hit. He wanted to start the truck and jerk out of the driveway and race to the hospital, but if it hurt her for him to touch her with just the pressure of his fingers, riding in the truck was going to be torture. He didn't have to start off that way. So he waited, sick, until she slowly straightened again.

He started the truck and backed out, trying to get all the turning done before another contraction started.

He tried to think. It was so much harder to be calm when he was emotionally invested.

"We should be timing those. Timing how close they are and timing how long they last," he said, grateful that some of his training at least kicked in. He didn't usually lose his head in an emergency.

But he hadn't been thinking with the rational side of his brain. He'd been thinking with the emotional side, which he didn't even realize he had. This was a nice time for it to show up.

During the next contraction, they were driving down the highway, and when he hit a bump, she moaned.

It was the first sound he heard her make, and it ripped at his chest. Yeah, he definitely wasn't going to be able to handle this. Couldn't handle hearing her in pain.

Probably, the hospital was used to men who needed to be

tranquilized because hearing their women suffer was just too much. They probably had some good drugs on hand just for the dads.

He thought about the fire station and the ambulance bays next to it where the EMTs hung out. If he weren't in such a big hurry, he'd swing by and request some good drugs. It was only half a joke.

His fingers squeezed the steering wheel as Reagan moaned once more. His hazard lights were on, and he was driving way too fast, but he was really hoping he wasn't going to end up delivering this baby along the road.

He didn't want to have to deliver the baby anywhere. He wanted Reagan to be comfortable in a hospital bed with lots of good drugs for herself, and some for him, and they could make silly jokes while the baby just appeared magically out of thin air.

He thought that wasn't quite the way it was going to work. It was a nice fantasy. Especially right now.

After what seemed like an interminable amount of time, he screeched to a halt so close to the emergency room doors they automatically opened because of his tire sitting on the sensor.

Someone could tow his truck away; he was fine with that.

He jumped out, grabbing her bag and racing around. She got the door open and one foot out, but she curled up again and held immeasurably still.

"Isn't there some kind of breathing you're supposed to be doing?" Did she take classes? He thought he remembered her talking about going to classes and her learning about Lamaze breathing. But it was hard to think, and he just couldn't remember.

As she slowly straightened, she said, "I know you're trying to be helpful with the whole breathing thing, but please don't."

She sounded very civil and kind, but she had one eye narrowed, and he wasn't sure he liked the look in her eye.

His eyes swept her up and down, looking for sharp objects.

He'd heard horror stories of worse, although typically it was the father of the baby who had the wrath of the mother directed at him. He was just an innocent bystander.

He didn't want to be an innocent bystander. He wanted to have the right to stand beside her.

He wished he had made sure of that during their last conversation, instead of putting it off.

At that thought, fear sliced through him.

People died in childbirth all the time. Certainly, he'd heard enough stories from the EMTs he hung out with at the fire station to know that it was more common than normal people knew.

"I'm sorry. No breathing. No touching," he said. "Please. Walk in the hospital. Please."

He'd resorted to begging, but he felt like it was worth it when she started to walk through the open doors.

Thankfully it was a small hospital, and they weren't busy. They'd already been seen, and someone was coming with a wheelchair.

"Labor?" the white-haired nurse wearing pink and blue scrubs asked.

He nodded, recognizing the nurse from his work at the fire station and as a part-time EMT. He couldn't remember her name.

The woman wasn't looking at him. Her eyes were on Reagan. She was nodding.

"What's the name of your doctor? Have you called them?" She put her arm around Reagan and guided her into the wheelchair.

Reagan and she talked. He felt like an extra unnecessary appendage but was determined to follow and make sure that Reagan was being taken care of in the very best way possible when the nurse looked up at him and said, "Sir, you need to—" Her eyes widened. "Andrew? I'm sorry, I didn't recognize you." She looked from Andrew back to Reagan, then down to the bag that Andrew carried, and back between them. "I didn't realize you...had someone." Obviously, she didn't think they were married and wasn't sure what to term the relationship.

He wasn't either. He wasn't going to get into it now.

Thankfully her name tag was visible. "Yeah. Thanks, Janet." He couldn't deny that he was with Reagan. If she'd let him stay beside her, he would. He could stand it.

"Okay," Janet said, all business again. "You know how to get up to the maternity floor, use the west elevators. But first, you need to move your truck. If an ambulance comes in, they're not going to be able to get through." Her professional demeanor cracked, and she gave a little smile. "You know that."

He knew a lot of things that he'd forgotten in the heat of the moment. When an emergency was going on around him, he could be impersonal and analytical, but with Reagan, he completely melted down, apparently, and had basically forgotten everything he knew.

Thankfully, he'd remembered how to drive at least.

"Thanks. I'll be right up."

She nodded and looked up to see a woman in a white lab coat walking out from the vending machine area.

"Oh, there's Hilary." She sounded relieved and glanced at Andrew. "You know, Reagan's midwife."

He had no idea. But he watched as Hilary greeted Reagan and then introduced herself to him, holding out her hand. He shook it, and Reagan didn't correct her when Hilary assumed he was with her. He didn't either. Although he didn't have the excuse of a contraction, and maybe that's why Reagan didn't say anything.

He didn't care. He was going to take advantage of it if he could.

"I'll be right up after I move my truck."

Hilary nodded and grabbed ahold of the wheelchair handles, stuffing the bag of chips in her lab coat pocket and a bottle of soda under her arm.

"I think you probably have time. First babies usually aren't fast. But we'll get her up and get her checked, then have a better idea of what's going to happen tonight."

Hilary's voice was calm and soothing, and although Andrew wasn't calm or soothed, he felt slightly less anxious. He still trotted outside, jumped in his truck, and parked haphazardly in the first available spot.

He was more familiar with the hospital across town, and he ended up going up the wrong elevator the first time, coming back down, and waiting forever for the elevator that he needed to come down and open.

Why they built the hospital with two separate three-story towers connected by a one-story bridgeway, he had no idea. But the only way to get from one third story to the other was to go back down the elevator, walk across the bridgeway, and go up the next.

It felt like forever 'til he finally got to the correct third floor, and the elevator doors opened.

As they opened, painful-sounding, ear-blocking, make-him-want-to-throw-himself-out-of-the-window screaming shrilled through the air, and he almost didn't step off the elevator.

That fifteen minutes he'd been gone had really changed things for Reagan.

It made him want to go cut the baby out himself.

Couldn't they do something for her?

Maybe the look on his face was a little frightening, or perhaps it was the way he strode, or power walked, to the nurses' station and briskly requested, "Where's Reagan?" because the nurse's eyes widened as the woman who'd been screaming drew breath, and there were two seconds of blissful silence before the bloodcurdling, ear-wrenching, throat-tearing, inhumane noise started again.

Andrew tried to remember what he'd learned about Lamaze breathing. Not because he wanted to tell Reagan about it, but because he needed it himself in order to be able to feel like he was not going to pass out through that animalistic sound.

He hadn't even realized Reagan was capable of making such a sound. He hadn't realized *any* human was capable of making such a sound. He assumed it was human anyway.

Even with all the accidents he'd been at as fire chief, the sound was beyond anything he'd experienced, and that was saying something.

He cringed. This helpless I-can't-do-anything-for-her feeling coated his insides with hot tar.

"Follow me," the nurse said, coming out from behind the desk and walking toward the sound.

Christmas decorations dangled from the ceiling, and there was a small tree in the waiting room they passed, but Andrew barely noticed.

He wasn't sure he could stay in the same room with that noise. With that painful sound. Well, part of him wasn't sure, but the greater part of him couldn't get there fast enough. He couldn't help, couldn't do anything, couldn't fix it, but he could at least be there. Maybe that was worth more than anything right now anyway.

The nurse turned left and entered a room, and the screaming wasn't quite as loud.

Andrew's gaze took in the figure on the bed, the quiet figure. Reagan. She was curled up on her side, already in a hospital gown, and totally silent. Her body stiff.

There was a band around her middle, and an IV had been started in her arm.

She didn't move, didn't make a sound, while the monitor line had gone straight up and stayed at the top as the screen scrolled past.

He assumed that was measuring the strength of the contraction, and he figured it probably depended on the placement of the belt, but it was still a little awe-inspiring to watch, because it looked like a granddaddy of all contractions.

Finally the line started coming down, and Reagan lifted her head.

"Andrew?" she said softly.

The screaming out in the hall continued, and Andrew's entire body felt cool and relaxed, knowing it wasn't Reagan. Maybe that was selfish.

"Are you okay, sweetie? You need me to get you anything while you're waiting for the anesthesiologist?" the nurse said, patting Reagan's hip. "Looks like you're going to have a Christmas baby, girl. Clock just struck midnight."

Reagan nodded her head and stiffened.

The nurse looked at Andrew. "There are ice chips on the tray. Don't give her anything else. I'll be back in a bit, once the anesthesiologist shows up. We got him out of bed." She said that last like maybe the anesthesiologist wasn't going be very happy to have been rousted out of bed this early on Christmas morning.

"Thanks," Andrew said, waiting for the nurse's footsteps to fade before he went down on one knee beside the bed, taking her hand in his and brushing her hair back away from her face with his other. "Do you mind if I'm here?"

"Please. I'm scared."

"The nurse wouldn't have walked out if she thought there was any problem."

"I know. Hilary said the same thing. She's got someone else who's a little bit more demanding than me apparently."

Andrew grimaced. The screaming woman.

"She went to take care of her and said I'd be fine." She swallowed, and her face worked, like she was trying to keep the fear off it. "I don't feel fine."

"I don't think you're supposed to feel fine. I think this is supposed to hurt. And be scary. I'll make sure everything goes the way it's supposed to."

He felt like he was lying through his teeth. He had no clue what was supposed to happen. Cheyenne had gone to stay with her mother two weeks before her due date with each of their boys. Again, probably for good reasons, in hindsight, but despite the fact that he had two boys, he wasn't nearly as experience in this as he should have been.

"Please don't leave me."

Like he could. That was an easy promise. "I won't. I'm staying."

"Another one. They're so much worse." She didn't say any more, but stiffened again, and squeezed his hand.

He glanced at the monitor, seeing the line go up, hit the top, and ride there. He turned away, making a mental note not to watch that thing anymore.

After what felt like a really long time, her body slowly relaxed. She opened her eyes. "They told me it would go faster if I got up and walked around, especially before the doctor gets here, but I didn't want to do it on my own."

"I'm here. If you want, we'll walk."

"I do. And I know you're right about the breathing, it just hurt so much, even breathing hurts." Her brows wrinkled, and her eyes were sad. "I'm sorry I snapped at you."

"You didn't snap. You were just putting me in my place, and you did it gently, being careful of my delicate, tender feelings. I appreciate that."

His attempt to joke turned her lips up a little. "I suppose laughing would probably make this go just as fast as walking. And might be more enjoyable. Tell me another joke."

"Sorry. Fresh out," he said automatically, even while racking his brain trying to think of something he could say that would make her smile. He hadn't had too much to laugh about today, himself. "I think everyone thinks this is my kid. It's not exactly a joke, but I do see humor there. And I haven't tried to tell anyone any different, because I thought they might not let me stay with you."

"Me either. Thank you," she said, stiffening again.

He waited until it was over. "I can't think of any jokes, but we could make a friendly wager on whether Athena and Preston will kill each other before we get home."

That got a weak smile out of her. "You asked Preston to come?" she asked with a fake horrified expression.

He nodded. "He'll balance Athena. She'd starch their underwear if he weren't there."

Reagan giggled. The sound made his heart sigh.

But then she grew more serious. "You know they don't get along? And you asked them both to come anyway?"

"They used to get along just fine. Athena used to babysit Preston and me. But since Shane died and Preston buried himself in the bottle, she can hardly stand to be around him."

"Nice. Is my brother safe? Or are they going to wheel him in and room him next to me?"

"If they do, I'll keep you updated on each other's progress."

"That's not making me feel better." She'd almost lost the lines between her eyes before she stiffened as another contraction shot the line on the little monitor up.

Still, he was encouraged that he'd been able to get some words and a smile out of her, so when the contraction went down, he tried for more.

He couldn't help with the pain, but maybe he could make the time go faster.

Whether or not it worked for her, he couldn't say, but he'd lost track of time when they were interrupted by the anesthesiologist.

It didn't provide immediate relief, but eventually Reagan was able to sleep, and he did too. By 7 o'clock on Christmas morning, Hilary was encouraging Reagan to push, and everything got a whole lot more real for Andrew.

He couldn't help her with this either, but she held his hand and curled over her stomach, her hair straggly and her face red, and as the hours went by, she became more and more exhausted, until he ended up being a cheerleader and encouraged her as she seemed to grow weaker and weaker.

He tried to meet Hilary's eyes more than once toward the end, wanting to ask with a raised brow if this was normal. He wanted relief for Reagan.

How long it would take? When was it going to end? When were they going to give up and give Reagan a break, taking the baby for her?

But Hilary seemed just as serene as she'd been all night and all morning, and he figured he'd worry when she did.

Finally Hilary said she saw the baby's head, which seemed to give Reagan a shot of energy, and she labored with a renewed vigor.

He supposed he shouldn't have been surprised when the baby, wet and slimy and shiny, slipped from her body, and Hilary barely held it before she laid it on Reagan's stomach.

"Meet your daughter, sweetheart," Hilary said, which, after the night of pain and the hours of ceaseless work and the sweat and the tears and everything else she'd been through, maybe shouldn't have made Reagan cry.

But it did. Not sobs, but her eyes filled and spilled over.

Happy tears, he was pretty sure, because he thought she wouldn't consider the wet and awkwardly-shaped bundle on her stomach to be anything but strikingly beautiful.

"She has your nose. And your cheeks. It's amazing how much of you I can see in her," he said softly. And he meant every word. He didn't think he could call the baby beautiful, but she looked so much like Reagan he was tempted.

Reagan touched her reverently, running a finger over her cheek and down her narrow ribs and checking her fingers and toes, smiling and laughing and looking at him through her tears. "Isn't she gorgeous?"

"Like her mother." Someone might find the irony in that, looking at Reagan with her sweat-streaked face, red and blotchy, dark circles under her eyes, and stringy hair, but he meant it, and when Hilary handed him the scissors to cut the cord, he wasn't sure if he'd ever felt more honored about anything in his life.

They took the baby away to wash and wrap her, weigh and measure her, and whatever else they did with babies.

Reagan squeezed his hand. "Thank you. I'm not sure I could've done that without you."

He wanted to laugh and say he didn't do anything, but he smoothed her hair back away from her forehead and said instead, "That was the most beautiful thing I've ever seen in my entire life. You were amazing."

She smiled, huge but tired, and maybe he shouldn't have done it, but he bent down and kissed her, gratified when she kissed him back.

Chapter Nineteen

Two days later, Reagan again sat beside Andrew in the pickup, only this time they were driving home from the hospital, and Esme rode in the back strapped into her baby carrier.

"You talked to Dylan? He still alive?"

Andrew grunted a laugh. "He's still alive. Athena wasn't there the whole time. Mr. Hudson isn't doing well, and although she traded some of her shifts, she was needed at the Hudsons' house."

Reagan had heard that. Violet had come to see her, along with some other ladies from Cowboy Crossing, and some of the whispered words had been that Mr. Hudson wasn't expected to make it into the new year.

Which, of course, made Reagan sad. A birth and a death. Life went on.

Celebrations and sad remembrances.

Heartbreak and a heart so full of love she wasn't sure what to do with it.

She'd never felt that overwhelming feeling of absolute adoration that she felt for Esme. Except...her eyes slid over to Andrew. It was a different type of feeling, but something as strong, maybe stronger, seemed to form between them as they shared her labor and Esme's birth.

She hadn't wanted to say anything about it. Because maybe it was the pregnancy hormones. Nurses had warned her that she would be going through mood shifts, and maybe what she felt, she was feeling alone, and he didn't share.

Andrew didn't go around kissing just anyone.

Their arrival home was met with cheers from the men in the house. Athena was with Mr. Hudson, but she'd left a gift basket and food in the fridge. She was nothing if not efficient and organized and probably exactly what Mrs. Hudson needed right now.

Preston didn't seem to appreciate Athena's talents and complained about her several times under his breath even while he cooed over Esme, but he took his leave soon, and they spent the afternoon in the living room with Reagan on the couch while Uncle Ron and Dylan fought with Andrew over who got to hold the baby.

Eventually Uncle Ron and Dylan went to bed, and Esme started to cry.

"So is that what she's going to do? Sleep all day and cry at night?" Andrew asked softly as he gently bounced her and her sobs subsided.

"I hope not. Although I have six weeks off, so I guess she can sleep whenever she wants to for six weeks."

"Then you're going back to work?"

"I have to." She gave him a lopsided grin. "My landlord's pretty demanding, and I'd be afraid to be late with the rent."

He didn't say anything for a while. He stood and bounced Esme for another five or ten minutes while Reagan laid her head back and closed her eyes.

It had only been a couple of days, and she was exhausted. She wasn't sure she was going to be able to do this.

She opened her eyes when she felt pressure on her leg. Andrew knelt beside her. Her eyes shifted to see Esme lying quietly in her bassinet, and she looked back at Andrew, her brows lifted.

"This probably isn't the best time, and you don't have to answer me right away. But we'd kind of talked about where we're going, and I know you said you're afraid I would go off doing dangerous things and eventually leave you, and I have to acknowledge that fear is based in reality, and I understand that."

He stroked his fingers over her hand. "And I guess we haven't known each other too long. Maybe you don't trust me, but I wanted to promise you that I won't do that. And following that promise, I wanted to say that I love you. I've loved you for a while, and I've just been too much of a coward to say it. I didn't want to waste any more time. I wanted you to know it."

She opened her mouth to return the sentiment, because she'd known for a while that she loved him, but he held his hand up.

"Please wait. I want to be long term with you. I want permanence. I get that you might not be ready for that, and I understand. But when you are, I'm talking marriage. I want to be a father to Esme and a family with Dylan too. I'm hoping you want the same."

He lifted her hand and kissed her knuckles, his eyes downcast, like he was studying the back of her hand.

"So, were you asking me to marry you or just announcing that you wanted to?"

She kinda had her head tilted, and maybe there was a little bit of humor lurking in her eyes, because as he looked up, he gave a guilty grin.

"That was a lot of information, wasn't it? I guess I didn't feel like you're ready for me to ask. I just wanted you to know where I stood. If you're ready, it was definitely a marriage proposal. I'm sorry it was so badly handled."

"Nothing else in my life this year has gone the way I planned it. I think that was pretty much a perfect marriage proposal. And I want to tell you I love you, and I'll marry you, whenever you want."

"Tomorrow?" he asked, only half joking.

"Tonight yet, if you can arrange it and Esme cooperates."

"We'll figure something out." Gladys pushed between them, and Andrew lifted his arm so she could put her nose and head in without him letting go of Reagan's hands.

"Sorry, girl. You're part of the family too."

Leaning forward, he kissed Reagan, despite the dog between them.

Epilogue

Mr. Hudson had chosen a pretty crappy week to die.

Preston shoved a hand in his pocket and leaned against the doorframe that led from the Hudson's kitchen to their living room.

He supposed Mr. Hudson hadn't had much say in the matter.

Death didn't really ask anyone's permission before snatching them away, out of this world and into the next, here one moment, then gone.

Man, he needed a drink.

He hadn't expected the line of visitors to be this long. Sure, he'd known the Hudson's were a beloved and respected family in Cowboy Crossing, but they'd gotten a foot of snow last night. The whole state should be shut down for a week.

But somehow people had managed to make it out.

The viewing was supposed to go from nine to eleven this morning. It was one, and he'd just set foot in the living room.

At this rate, Andrew and Reagan would have to move their wedding, scheduled for four pm at the white church in Cowboy Crossing to a different day.

Preston wasn't much more interested in going to a wedding than he was a funeral.

It meant a whole day with no alcohol.

You need to quit anyway.

He hated that voice in his head.

You might as well have died with Shane as much as you are wasting your life.

Didn't he know it.

Mrs. Hudson stood at the head of the casket. Her face pinched and tired, but serene.

The woman would look serene during an air raid, probably. But part of her calmness could be attributed to Athena, who stood like part stoic solider, part best friend, next to her.

Athena was just the kind of person that anyone would want to have beside them, anytime, but especially at a trying time like this.

Her dark hair was pulled back and piled high on her head. She looked sleek and sophisticated, yet approachable as she shook an older gentleman's hand and guided him away from Mrs. Hudson. She was keeping close track, and making sure Mrs. Hudson didn't overdo it.

A natural nurturer. She also was a take-charge type and a bossy know-it-all.

She looked up, her blue eyes piercing across the distance that separated them. He had to force himself to not turn away. He hated the judgement that he could feel coming from her.

Not that she'd ever said anything. Not that she even looked like she was judging him. He could just feel it, because of course she was. How could she not? He was judging himself.

He needed to give up the bottle and stop wasting his life.

But, without alcohol, the pain hurt too bad. The bottle's pull, stronger than his self-control, was irresistible.

Athena's lips pulled in and for a moment something like regret crossed her face along with another emotion that in a regular person he might term affection or something more.

Not Athena. Drill sergeants didn't have feelings.

Several hours later his best friend on this earth stood before a small crowd of people and pledged his life to the mother of the baby that Preston had somehow become responsible for holding.

He was pretty sure it was wet. And about to cry. Panic, like he'd never felt on any climb, screamed in his chest. Trying to keep his gaze relaxed and cool, he scanned the assembled guests from where he stood behind Andrew.

Every eye was fixed on the groom as he lowered his head to kiss his new bride. No one was paying attention to the only groomsman, nor the bundle getting ready to explode in his arms.

The little pixie face scrunched up.

The panic grabbed his throat with both hands.

His eyes, wide open and no longer cool, but probably showing every ounce of his complete terror, darted around the room.

With Andrew leaning over, making this the longest wedding kiss Preston had ever sat or stood through, Athena, behind Reagan, was clearly visible.

She was the only person in the church who didn't have their eyes glued on that really long, really deep, really barely PG-13 kiss. Holy smokes. Were they going for a world record, or something? How long did wedding kisses usually take?

He needed to get this kid out of his arms before she brought the house down.

Just because he was completely incompetent around children, didn't mean he wanted the world to know.

Cheers went up as Andrew lifted his head. Preston got ready to step forward to hand him his baby.

But, holy smokes, he lowered his head again!

Athena lifted a brow at his horror struck expression. He was sure this had never happened before.

Athena's lips pursed and her eyes narrowed before she gathered her dress in one hand and moved out from behind Reagan, stepping carefully around the kissing couple and over to him.

"Trade me," she said, holding out the hand that held a bouquet of some kind of yellow and blue flowers.

He wanted to say no. Wanted to tell her he was fine and could handle a little ten pound human for ten minutes.

But he wasn't and he couldn't and he didn't.

Without a word, he handed her over, ignoring the flash of heat that kicked up his arm when Athena's hands brushed his arm.

Maybe he'd wondered what it would be like for someone to not just take care of him, but to care about him.

Maybe he'd like to clash with her forceful personality and feel the sparks they were sure to produce.

But it wasn't going to happen.

He'd give up the bottle for her – he knew he needed to, but he wasn't giving up his daredevil ways, and become a boring and predictable family man.

Athena wouldn't be happy with anything less.

———

Join Jessie's list and be the first to know about new releases and sales on her books!

Read My Dearest Athena, formerly called His Best Friend's Sister in the Show Me State, the last book in the Cowboy Crossing series. Athena and Preston's story features the brother's best friend trope! Keep reading for a sneak peek now.

A Gift from Jessie

View this code through your smart phone camera to be taken to a page where you can download a FREE ebook when you sign up to get updates from Jessie Gussman! Find out why people say, "Jessie's is the only newsletter I open and read" and "You make my day brighter. Love, love, love reading your newsletters. I don't know where you find time to write books. You are so busy living life. A true blessing." and "I know from now on that I can't be drinking my morning coffee while reading your newsletter – I laughed so hard I sprayed it out all over the table!"

Claim your free book from Jessie!

Escape to more faith-filled romance series by Jessie Gussman!

The Complete Sweet Water, North Dakota Reading Order:

Series One: Sweet Water Ranch Western Cowboy Romance (11 book series)

Series Two: Coming Home to North Dakota (12 book series)

Series Three: Flyboys of Sweet Briar Ranch in North Dakota (13 book series)

Series Four: Sweet View Ranch Western Cowboy Romance (10 book series)

Spinoffs and More! Additional Series You'll Love:

Jessie's First Series: Sweet Haven Farm (4 book series)

Small-Town Romance: The Baxter Boys (5 book series)

Bad-Boy Sweet Romance: Richmond Rebels Sweet Romance (3 book series)

Sweet Water Spinoff: Cowboy Crossing (9 book series)

Small Town Romantic Comedy: Good Grief, Idaho (5 book series)

True Stories from Jessie's Farm: Stories from Jessie Gussman's Newsletter (3 book series)

Reader-Favorite! Sweet Beach Romance: Blueberry Beach (8 book series)

Blueberry Beach Spinoff: Strawberry Sands (10 book series)

From Strawberry Sands to: Raspberry Ridge (12 book series)

Swoonfully Jolly Holiday Stories:

Holiday Romance: Cowboy Mountain Christmas (6 book series)

Cowboy Mountain Christmas Spinoff: A Heartland Cowboy Christmas (9 book series)

New and Much Loved: Mistletoe Meadows (4 books and counting!)

Laughing Through the Snow: Christmas Tree, PA Sweet Romcoms (6 short reads)